MISCHIEVOUS PRINCE

CAPTURED BY A DRAGON-SHIFTER SERIES

MICHELLE M. PILLOW

MICHELLE M. PILLOW® - MICHELLEPILLOW.COM

Welcome to the dangerous world of Qurilixen where dragon-shifters and cat-shifters rule as fiercely as they love.

He's a dragon-shifting prince, and she's a human. What could possibly go wrong?

Dragon-shifter Prince Finn will do whatever it takes to save his people from extinction, even if that means sneaking through a portal to Earth to find a bride. With dragon men disappearing and threats to cut off their supply to eligible women, he knows the portal is their only hope of survival. And it might be his only chance to find love.

"First meets are easy. Staying is hard."

Food blogger, Sadie Harcourt isn't one for commitment. Her job offers the perfect excuse to keep moving. Never did she expect that her love of adventure would accidentally catapult her from Faulkner Alley in Oxford, Mississippi onto a planet of Alpha shifters looking to marry.

When the elders discover that Finn accessed the portal, all hell breaks loose. Factions pounce on the opportunity to overthrow the royal family. Now everything he holds dear rests in the hands of a captivating woman who arrived on his planet by mistake.

Lords of the Var® Series
The Savage King
The Playful Prince
The Bound Prince
The Rogue Prince
The Pirate Prince

Captured by a Dragon-Shifter Series
Determined Prince
Rebellious Prince
Stranded with the Cajun
Hunted by the Dragon
Mischievous Prince
Headstrong Prince

Space Lords Series
His Frost Maiden
His Fire Maiden
His Metal Maiden
His Earth Maiden

His Woodland Maiden

Dynasty Lords Series
Seduction of the Phoenix
Temptation of the Butterfly

To learn more about the Qurilixen World series of
books and to stay up to date on the latest book list
visit www.MichellePillow.com

NOTE FROM AUTHOR

IF YOU'RE new to my books, the *Dragon Lords* are my bestselling futuristic shape-shifter romance series. The stories became reader favorites, and so I wrote things from their enemy's point of view in a spin-off series for the cat-shifting *Lords of the Var*®. Then they ventured off into the stars in the series installment *Space Lords*. Now, I'm time traveling with them back to our time with the series *Captured by a Dragon-Shifter*, which you are now reading book one of. Don't worry, I have the series reading order on my website to help you figure it all out, http://michellepillow.com/.

To those of you *not* new to my books, readers have emailed asking Dragon Lords cultural questions since the first dragon-shifting prince released years ago. I have teased you with a lot of little hints of how the Draig found brides in "the old days". Many of you have expressed wanting to climb aboard the space ship and sail away into the future—which would probably take some cryogenic freezing and a lot of icy waiting. Well, before you start packing those sweaters... I don't want any of you going to that extreme, so I've brought your favorite dragon-shifters and cat-shifters to modern-day Earth. They don't live on our planet, but they have recently started to revisit.

For *Dragon Lords* and *Lords of the Var*® fans, *Captured by a Dragon-Shifter* is a modern-day prequel series to those first books. They take place long before the princes you know and love ever found their mates, long before *The Dragon's Queen*, in a time when the dragon-shifters and cat-shifters actually—wait for it—*liked* each other and hung out as friends. They also don't have Galaxy Brides to bring them women. There's no one left to marry on the planet and things are starting to get desperate.

Author recommends reading series installments in order of release for the simple fact she likes hiding little tidbits in the books as she goes and it's more fun that way, though each book can be read as a standalone if you prefer.

To my new hometown.
Hotty Toddy!

DRAIG NORTHERN MOUNTAINS, PLANET OF QURILIXEN

"ADMIT IT, IVAR, YOU'RE INTRIGUED." Prince Finn hoped his mischievous smile and lighthearted approach would convince his good friend to relax. Most cat-shifters were known for their untamed ways, but not Prince Ivar of the Var. If Finn hadn't known the man since childhood, he would have been intimidated by Ivar's frozen, stoic expression, and dead stare.

"This is highly irregular." Ivar folded his arms over his chest. "We should not be meeting like this before the royal assembly with the elders."

Finn's expression fell. For a cat-shifter, the man was uptight and lacked any sense of adventure. He would have preferred Ivar's more carefree brother for this plan, but Rafe had married already and wouldn't be of any help. Ivar and Finn were the only unmated princes left on the planet.

The soft green-blue light of evening threw shadows over the valley. It wouldn't get too much darker. With three suns, the planet was cast in almost constant daylight. Finn liked the stillness of the valley, the gentle sway of the yellow-tinted grasses.

"I love our home world," Finn sighed in frustration. "I love my people. This is where I want to raise a family. I would do nothing to jeopardize any of this. And that is why I will fight for this place and my people."

Finn's words seemed to hang in the air. Ivar didn't move.

"Gods bones, Ivar," Finn swore, losing all pleasantry. "You know what will happen at that meeting—our parents and the elders will close the portal to Earth. They will demand it buried under a mountain so deep that no one will ever remember that it's there. What do we tell our people in a hundred years? In three hundred? When our parents are gone, and they are looking at us to fix things as the last of shifter kind is dying out because the one viable option we had to find them wives was closed due to fear mongers and political maneuverings."

"Do you think their fears are unjustified? Already dragons have been sneaking through to Earth and not returning. You worry about the population? Yours is walking off this planet willingly. How many men have you lost to that portal? How many slip through and do not come back home? How many want to but can't come back, or don't know how? Each night it opens in a different location. We do not want to see our cat-shifter population dwindle over promises of a better life on Earth, promises you and I both know are exaggerated. Humans have not changed. You saw their films glorifying alien destruction. You have seen their taverns and their streets. They cannot even feed their own kind. People whisper that the portal leads to some great valley full of unmated woman waiting with open arms. We both know that is not the truth, but a false hope spread by opportunists."

"We opened the portals with the plan that we would show them it could work. All four of us would go through and find mates. Kyran and Rafe have succeeded. We at least have to try. If all four princes show a united front. If we prove to the people that Earth women will come if we do it correctly. If we—"

"I seem to remember you not being all that eager to marry the first night we went through," Ivar interrupted. "Or the several times after that. It was a game to you. You had your chance. You could have grabbed any number of women if that is what you wanted."

"I thought we'd have more time to decide. What is wrong in wanting to have a little fun first? Everyone says that when you see your mate you'll know. I've not felt anything concrete." Finn sighed. "I'm still waiting for the gods to speak to me. And I know you're waiting for them to speak to you. No man seeks a lonely life."

"I am not convinced the voices of our gods can be heard on Earth," Ivar stated. "There is too much noise, too much clutter."

"They spoke to our brothers." Finn took a deep breath and closed his eyes. He wasn't telling his friend the whole plan. He wouldn't. Not yet. Not until they were through the portal and on the other side. "Ivar, I'm asking you to come with me tonight. Let us prove this portal is a solution, not a problem."

Ivar's eyes turned toward the sky as if he contemplated the wide space beyond. "We have been building relations with alien cultures through our intergalactic contacts."

"Any that are compatible with shifters?" Finn questioned. The Draig did not like associating with space travelers. Often, the only reason aliens landed was because they wanted something—to steal resources, to sell their religions, or to take advantage of the locals.

"I'm not saying I don't think the portals could work, but..." Ivar's scowl deepened.

"What?"

Ivar lifted his chest. "I think they are mismanaged. If the portals were under Var guard, people would not be slipping through. They would be regulated."

"The valley entrance is locked. There are only a few keys. The palace entrance is guarded and reachable through a long tunnel." This was not the conversation Finn wanted to be having—a debate between royal families. "It could have been one of your guards, as easily as it was one of ours, that let the men through. That's what happens when you tell men you have the solution to their biggest problem but aren't ready to share it with them. Our parents and the elders are too busy arguing over the details, but nothing is being done. Now they want to close it because it's easier than dealing with it."

"You did not call me to this valley to argue." Ivar motioned to the cave. "I assume you want to go to Earth to look for brides?"

"Yes." Finn lifted two satchels from the ground.

"I checked the charts and brought us supplies. We're going to," he paused, having to focus on the word to pronounce the foreign name, "*Miss-is-sip-pie.*"

"And you think that if I go with you to Miss Pie, and we both bring back the women ordained by the gods to be our wives, we can show up at that meeting and convince the elders and our parents to keep the portals open?"

"Yes. If they see that we are well matched."

"Why will this trip be any different from the others?"

"The gods will bless us. I know they will. We need this. Our people's future needs this."

"And if they don't?" Ivar cut straight to the point as always. "You know the odds are against us."

Finn stiffened and forced himself to meet Ivar's gaze. "Then we make them bless us."

Ivar arched a brow. "You want to lie about the will of the gods? You would be willing to spend an eternity with a woman who was not your true mate?"

Finn nodded. "If it means the survival of the Draig, then yes, I will make that sacrifice. No one will ever know the truth beyond the two of us."

Ivar's mouth curled up at the side. It wasn't a smile so much as approval. The look took Finn by surprise since the man rarely showed approval of anything. "I did not think you had it in you to put our people before yourself. I misjudged you. Yes. I will go with you tonight to bring back brides so that we may ensure the future of our population. I will make this sacrifice with you. We will take half mates and never let a moment's unhappiness show. But I want something in return."

Finn was not delusional in believing that tonight would be special. Dropping the pretense of destined mates and love didn't make that knowledge any easier. "What?"

"Once we do this, we push for regulations for portal travel. We stop the flow of shifter defectors before the cats join the dragons. Staying on Earth cannot be an option."

Finn nodded. "Agreed. The Draig have discussed only going on the one night of Qurilixian darkness a year and making it a mass wedding celebration. It can become a ritual. We go, get brides, bring them back and celebrate those who are chosen. Men will have to be trained before they can go through the portal. It will become a rite of passage."

"One earned through honor," Ivar added.

"And in twenty years no one will question the tradition."

"I want Var access to the portal. We will build an

embassy on Draig land, right here in the valley where both families will have a joint say over travel. My people need to know that we are not at the mercy of the dragons."

"And my people need to know the cats respect the fact that we have guarded these portals since our ancestors came here to escape Earth's tyranny. We took the risk by being the closest. If the human hunters ever found their way through, it was our people who would be the first in their path."

Ivar lifted his hand to take a satchel. "Then it is decided. Tonight, we enter through that portal to find brides by any means necessary."

Finn had never wanted his people to kidnap women. What if they didn't want to come? What if they were unhappy? What if he and Ivar never found peace in their marriages? They could be signing on for hundreds of years' worth of misery. Then again, what did the fate of four people mean when countered against the survival of thousands?

2

THE SQUARE, OXFORD, MISSISSIPPI

"How is it the weather is both chilly and humid at the same time? I didn't think that could be scientifically possible." Sadie Harcourt mustered a smile for the waitress before turning her attention to the street scene below as if the bright sunlight would hold the answer. She sat alone at a table in the middle of a balcony. On her left were rustic walls weathered by time and to her right open air.

"Just wait until the summer," the waitress laughed. Her soft Southern accent made everything she said sound genuine and friendlier than what Sadie was used to. "You'll feel like you're breathing in water." She set down a glass of ice water and left.

"I'll be gone before then," Sadie whispered.

That was one thing her life afforded—constant movement.

She made enough money on advertising from her travel food blog to keep her life adventurous. For the next three months, she'd be living near Oxford, tasting all the delicious fare Mississippi had to offer. Having scouted out the menus as she planned her work itinerary, she'd also be leaving Mississippi about fifty pounds heavier.

Sadie opened the digital notepad on her phone, and typed, "*Fried Food Nirvana,*" as a possible article title. Staring at it for a second, she deleted it. Not all ideas would be golden.

Three months was just long enough to explore the area and see the sights. She'd meet a few people and taste the culinary delights without getting too close for comfort.

"*Country Fried Reporter,*" she typed and then deleted. Dammit. Normally she had a collection of good story ideas by now.

Sadie's main goal in life was to feed her appetite for adventure, feast on people's cultures and customs, and enjoy their foods without hanging around long enough to become a local. Anthropologically speaking that made Sadie a vampire.

"*Vampire reporter sucks her own brain dry of*

ideas," she typed in her notes. *"As a society, you eat what you are, and I devour cultures. Developed societies boast of their advancement with an array of cuisines, fine dining to fast foods. And developing countries rely on customs to frame their meager but healthier diets."*

That idea she saved. She'd have to take out the vampire bit, but the rest was workable.

For now, Sadie was content in losing herself in all that the South had to offer—starting with Northern Mississippi, down through the Delta, and ending in Memphis. Since the iconic city sat on the border of three states, she was counting Memphis as part of her Mississippi tour.

She pulled out her laptop and personal Wi-Fi device to get a little work done while she waited. It wasn't a Wi-Fi-computer kind of restaurant, but no one at the other tables appeared to mind.

She opened a document entitled, *"Soul Food Tour of the South,"* but instead of writing further, she ended up staring at the historic courthouse below, beyond the wrought iron railing. The white building served as the center focus of The Square. It was located in the middle of an island, surrounded by a roundabout. She imagined the cars drove around it in circles, like sharks swimming a moat outside of a castle. Opposite the historic building, restaurants, bars, boutiques, and bookstores framed the picturesque setting.

Oxford seemed as nice of a place as any. And for a moment Sadie wondered what it would be like to live in one location.

As a child, her military father had been relocated almost yearly, taking her from post to post. When she moved out as a young adult, she kept traveling—three months here, six months there, crashing with someone who advertised for a roommate, extended stay hotels. She made no real friends because she was better with first meets and small talk.

Meeting people was easy. Sustaining a relationship was hard.

Sadie had smelled the fried green tomatoes before they appeared. The waitress set the plate down on the table. The woman mumbled something along the lines of, "I'll be right back with the rest of your order," before scrambling away.

Sadie turned her attention back to her surroundings. The restaurant had a history if the proud traditions displayed on the walls were any indication. The tin signs and authentic memorabilia looked like they'd hung on the exposed brick walls since the beginning of the last century. Framed posters boasted products from yesteryear that Sadie had never heard of, but could be dated to the early 1900s by the artwork.

All around her, couples—young and old—looked at each other knowingly as waiters and waitresses arrived with their orders. Visitors like Sadie watched while the legendary dishes immortalized on walls of social media materialized onto plates in front of them.

She could spend the next however long, maybe forever, eating her way around Oxford. Easily.

An intermittent draft pestered her until she had to pull her jacket off the back of her chair and throw it over her shoulders. A group of people walked below, initiating conversation with another group at a table next to the railing.

"Hotty Toddy!"

"Hotty Toddy, yourselves."

They yelled up and down at each other in greeting. Seconds later the waitress joined in on the loud conversation about football prospects, the team's chances, and the next great quarterback.

What would it be like to be a waitress in this restaurant, coming to the same job day after day for years, knowing nearly everyone who passed by? Or the owner of the restaurant? Generations of family members passing down their legacy.

Part of her always felt she was missing out on something everyone else took for granted. Oxford appeared to have those things—family, traditions, friends, and community pride.

Candy coated music wafted through the square, floating all around the fantastical setting, engulfing the citizens of Oxford in a vibe that lifted spirits and the mood of those who flocked there. The quaint college town had been likened to a bubble or an oasis, and some even went as far as to call it utopia.

She lifted her finger to the keyboard and paused as the conversation died down. A man at the nearby table explained the fine art of formal tailgating in support of the local college's football team. "… no, not on the tailgates of trucks, tents go up and down the entire grove like a small city… people pay to have it catered… now there is a business opportunity to be had if I didn't like going to the games and drinking beers so much."

Laughter erupted in favor of his statement.

"Everything all right?" The waitress motioned toward the untouched appetizer.

Sadie lifted her phone with a small laugh. She opened the camera app. "Photo op. Meals don't happen anymore unless they're posted on the Internet."

"Post away, be sure to tag us," the waitress said, before winking. "As long as you have something nice to say."

"Will do," Sadie said as the woman went about her business.

To keep her word, Sadie stood up and took a picture of the green fried tomato slices. A bright light flashed as she tapped the screen. The picture turned out distorted. She frowned, turning her phone over to see if something was covering the lens.

"What was that light?" the football fan stood and peered over the street below.

Sadie followed his gaze. Two men strode across the street on the opposite side of the square toward the courthouse lawn. They were dressed strangely, part medieval re-enactor, part gothic performer.

The tallest one wore a tank held together with cross lacing up the side and tight pants with matching cross laces along the thighs. The other had a looser tunic style shirt over dark pants and boots. They both carried a messenger-type bags strapped over their chests. Beyond their brown hair, she couldn't see much else.

"Ha, college towns," the football fan said to his

guests with a boisterous laugh. "Never know what you'll see."

The men moved onto the small patch of lawn and stopped to look around, their postures showing they were in serious conversation. One pointed into the distance and tried to walk. The other grabbed his arm and made a sweeping gesture toward the balcony diners. Sadie wasn't sure if it was curiosity or something else that made her stomach twitch with nervousness or her heart beat a little faster.

Sadie suddenly realized she was standing in the middle of the restaurant.

Slowly, as if it mattered, she lowered herself back into her seat, placed her phone down on the table, and swapped it for a fork. Her eyes remained in the direction of the courtyard to watch what the men would do next.

One of the men turned, and she felt her breath catch. A sweep of brown hair quickly covered the impression of dark eyes. Maybe she'd been daydreaming about normal for too long, and it had affected her, but she felt a strange pull toward the men, or to be exact, the one closest to her.

The moment felt so simple. First meets were easy. All Sadie had to do was stand up, walk down to the courtyard, and say hello. Then she would be part of that man's story, a part of whatever interesting thing he was doing on a weekday late afternoon.

She closed her laptop and slid it back into her bag. The fact she wanted to be a part of that man's story made her do exactly the opposite. She wouldn't seek him out. She'd stay on task for the day and do her job. Then, tomorrow, she'd do it again. And, in three months, she'd leave Oxford to start over.

3

"LET'S TRY THIS WAY. I see a crowd," Finn pointed toward a pack of humans passing by the opening of the tight passageway. "We'll have greater odds with more numbers."

He began to walk toward the humans when Ivar stopped him. "Look closer and remember what planet we're on. They are too young by human years." He gestured in the opposite direction.

Finn did a small circle as he reexamined the site. The short, narrow passageway where they landed gave little sense of a location and yet was exposed on both ends.

Only half of the passageway was covered from above. The corridor appeared to be made from two buildings. An "alleyway," if he remembered the human word correctly. If someone were to lean against the wall at the wrong time, they'd fall through to Qurilixen. A black door against a white wall marked the general area, and a sign in the passageway read, "Faulkner Alley," to mark the exact positioning of the magical location. He frowned as he looked at a skull hanging front and center on the door. "This does not feel like the safest place for a portal. If there had been more people someone might have seen us."

"Yes." Ivar pointed at the metal skull. "A torture chamber, or prison, perhaps? Either way, it is a clear warning that death awaits us if we go inside."

"It will work to protect this portal," Finn decided. "No one would seek death so readily as to come knocking on its door."

"That is probably why the scouts marked this location as safe for passage, but crossed it off their charts and said no one was to go through to this stop," Ivar answered. They didn't know enough about portal travel to change where the openings mani-fested. "We must take care. We cannot let anyone see us return home. We do not want to be responsible for the humans finding out our location and following us through."

"We didn't have a choice. We need to find wives

and don't have the luxury of waiting for pre-approved travel. The elders wouldn't agree if we were to ask permission first, and then we'd be defying an actual decree." Finn noticed several people had paused at the end of the passage and were staring at them. "I think no one saw us come through. They're curious, but no one appears panicked."

Ivar strode away from the inquisitive group looking at them and headed toward the end of the passageway before stepping out into the sunlight. Finn followed him, making a mental note where they were.

They were in a town. The tightly pressed building and balconies maximized space while blocking distant landscape views. People kept in small groups as they took the many paths winding around a central white building.

"To the rhythm, to the rhythm..."

The scene was just like in the intergalactic broadcasts his people had intercepted.

A green metallic flash in Ivar's eyes was the only giveaway of how surreal it was for the cat-shifter to be back on the planet Earth.

Finn once again found himself immersed in the blue orb's decadence, and its people's unashamed drive to have fun. A smile rested on his features momentarily as he surveyed his surroundings. The rush it gave him was exhilarating. A tingle worked its way over him. His armored shell broke the skin on the back of his hands and several other places on his body, but Finn eased himself back out of the transitory state before it was too late. He had to resist the urge to shift from all the excitement around him.

Careful not to let Ivar see how he felt, Finn swallowed the small lump forming in his throat as he watched the strange yet wonderful humans in their natural habitat.

Humans. They stood in doorways and sauntered about the place before settling in bars and restaurants where they feasted without worry or care for anything but themselves, looking vaguely out into the universe like no one else existed but them.

Their ignorance and passive veneer fascinated him. To Finn, they were shifters who could not shift. Prisoners of their fears, living in denial that there was anything beyond what they knew, until one day their minds could not live with the lie anymore. It was only a matter of time until some alien species made themselves known. It would not be the Draig or the Var, but it would happen.

Finn felt deeply for the *unshifted*. Their naivety and vulnerability made them even more attractive.

Finn shrugged off feelings of nostalgia and pity to resume his role as leader and savior of his people. Here on Earth he had one goal. To find a mate.

"We go there." Ivar continued walking, not giving Finn a choice but to follow. "Where people eat. Rafe found his woman in a food place and has had much luck in his marriage. We will go to those locations."

"Kyran found his woman in a tavern," Finn reminded Ivar. He pointed in the other direction. "I hear what could be one that way."

Ivar grabbed his arm to stop him. "We have been to many of those places. I believe your brother to be blessed that night because the gods saw we were new to the planet and lost. Those tavern women are not looking for mates. They are looking for fun."

"I like fun," Finn said.

"Do you forget why we're here?" Ivar's frown deepened. "This was your plan."

No. Finn hadn't forgotten, but it was amusing to poke at Ivar's serious nature. "Fine. We will look at food places."

Since they found themselves on grass rather than a sidewalk, Finn positioned his hand on the fence and leaped over it to land on the concrete. He heard Ivar do the same as they made their way toward the balconies where people dined. Cars moved past in the street. He'd learned his lesson about looking for cars on his first visit.

His eyes turned upward. A man stood, making giant motions with his arms before a group of spectators. Next to him was an empty table with dishes.

"We need to choose quickly so we have time to convince them to come," Ivar stated. "We will be cutting our time close, but we should wait for the evening before grabbing a woman to bring through."

"The universe didn't give us much time with these portals, did they? Not even a full day through, and about a year in between portal jumps to the same place. One night hardly seems like enough time for a proper courtship."

"Perhaps it is enough," Ivar countered. "Why would you need a year to understand what you should know in a moment? All shifters say it is the same. One look and they know."

"You don't think they exaggerate?" Finn didn't want to confess that he sometimes worried that part of him was broken. "We have seen so many women in our travels here, and not one has spoken to the shifter inside of me."

"Perhaps you question it too much," Ivar said.

"Besides, we're not here to find our mates. We're here to find any mate. This is not about us. It's about—"

"I know what it's about," Finn interrupted, aware of a father and daughter crossing the street toward them. "Now is not the place to discuss it. We're drawing attention."

He noted the painted boundaries the man kept his child within and took that same path across to the opposite sidewalk.

"Hello," a soft voice greeted.

Finn glanced down to the little girl and nodded his head uncomfortably. The child hugged closer to her father's leg. He knew little about children, especially female children. Since women weren't being born on his home world, Finn had little interaction with them. This one in a pink dress with her dark hair pulled up in a tight bun looked fragile. He thought it best not to step too close.

A low growl sounded behind him as Ivar acknowledged the child. The girl screamed and ran the rest of the way across the street. The father looked upset, but instead of facing Ivar he ran after the girl. It was a wise decision. The cat-shifter could be deadly in a fight, and a human would be no match for his claws.

"What was that?" Finn demanded.

Ivar actually looked confused by what had happened. "I growl at the Var children all the time. It makes them laugh. I think that one might be broken. Did you hear the noise she made?"

"Or she's human and doesn't know how to speak shifter," Finn countered. "Come. We need to hurry before that father turns back. And try not to scare any more locals, particularly their offspring."

"*Hotty Toddy!*" a man yelled down from the dining balcony.

Ivar stiffened, as if ready for a fight. He lifted his arms and put his back against Finn's. The battle cry was echoed several times down each of the side streets until finally it dissipated. The man on the balcony grinned in pride at the wave of sound he'd created as he sat down.

"We should leave," Ivar stated. "That man must be a commander. See how he stands above the others surveying the area from a vantage point?"

"I don't think that was a threat," Finn corrected, more curious than worried about this new location. "I see no one coming for us."

"Still, perhaps we should show respect to the reigning authorities." Ivar turned toward the balcony, placed a fist over his heart and bowed. Finn, slower to move, did the same. The balcony man laughed and pointed down at them before pushing to his feet and bowing in return. Under his breath, he said, "Let us retreat to another section of this town, away from that man's sight."

Walking around the human town proved to be a fruitless endeavor. All the women they saw were too young, too married, or too pre-mated to human males. None of them caused his inner shifter to surge forth to make claim. Still, Finn hoped he and Ivar would find their true mates, proof that the portal should remain open. That would be the simple route to solving the futures of their people.

The gods did not wish for their path to be easy.

At one point, Ivar had insisted they split up to look for women, and Finn let him go. Ivar could handle himself, and Finn wasn't worried about the cat-shifter prince. Besides, Ivar would be within shouting distance should trouble occur.

"I see you have had the same bad luck as I," Ivar stated. Though Finn had hoped it would be otherwise, the cat-shifter appeared at their meeting place alone. "The scouts were right to mark this location as unusable. There are no women of appropriate age to be had. All the ones I have seen unattached are too young. All those old enough appear to be wearing the Earth finger shackle."

"I found two," Finn said. "They're waiting for us at the portal."

"What?" Ivar glanced down the block in the direction they must take to get home. "Where?"

Finn nodded. "Yes. They're of the right age. They're pretty. They appear kind. They are perhaps a bit too delicate, but—"

"All Earth women are fragile. That is to be expected," Ivar put forth.

Finn gestured that they should move. "The hour turns late. They are waiting near the portal for us."

"I don't understand," Ivar's steps quickened as he headed toward Faulkner Alley. Finn wasn't sure if it was out of nervousness or excitement at the prospect of meeting his future. "How did you convince them to come?"

Finn grinned and motioned his hand. "What woman can resist the smooth charm of a dragon?"

Ivar's pace quickened. Finn hurried behind him. They crossed the circular street toward the central white building before again crossing to reach the shadowed passageway. The locals kept out of the shadowed pathway and instead stayed on the lighted streets.

Reaching the location of the portal, Ivar glanced inside the passage before searching along the side of the building. He then crossed through the passage and did the same thing on the other side. "Where are the women? You said you found women for us."

"They were excited. I bet they already found their way through." Finn motioned that Ivar should go inside. "Just beyond the black door. You should go in after them. The caves will be dark on the other side of the portal, and they might be frightened."

Ivar moved toward the portal. He glanced around to make sure no one watched as he lifted his hand. The tips of his fingers grazed the edge, activating a soft light for the barest of seconds. Finn held his breath and didn't move.

"Hey, are you guys in line for that secret grilled cheese place?" a young kid called down the alley. "I don't think you can get in this early."

Ivar jerked his hand back.

"No," Ivar and Finn said in unison.

"Oh, doesn't look like you're dressed for it anyway," the kid answered before going on his way.

"This place is odd," Ivar stated. He lowered his hand and didn't go through. He slowly turned toward Finn. His eyes narrowed, and he nodded toward the portal. "You first."

"What?" Finn gave a nervous laugh. "Go ahead. I'm right behind you."

"I insist." Ivar crossed his arms over his chest.

"It will close soon," Finn said. He reached to give Ivar a small push. "Stop playing around and go."

Ivar barely moved. "There are no women, are there?"

Finn thought about continuing his lie, but he needed to get Ivar through the portal to home. "No. You're right. There are not. I had hoped that fate would smile on us, and we'd find the ones we were meant to be with, but I wasn't forthcoming about the plan in coming here."

"Get in the portal. We will discuss this on our home world."

"I'm not going back. I'm staying for the next year. I need you to tell our parents they can't cave in the portals. I am a prince. They will not leave me behind. This is the only way to negotiate more time for our people. You know as well as I what the elders are going to demand at that meeting. They have been seeking an excuse to cut off Earth since the directions to the portal were first unearthed in the Draig royal library. They are scared of things that are no longer threats. Look at this world, Ivar." Finn swept his arms wide over the town. "There are no more shifter hunters. There are no more knights. There aren't even the castles the old ones talk about. We don't exist in this world but in fairy tales and fantasy. Convince them that this is for the best for both cats and dragons. When the portal to this place opens back up, I will be here, waiting."

"I'm not leaving you behind," Ivar denied. "How will you survive on this planet? I am looking around, and they are a primitive, strange people. They do not even acknowledge the existence of beings beyond their skies. How vain are these humans to think they are the only ones to crawl out of the infinite?"

"Your feelings are exactly why I didn't tell you my intentions. I had hoped it wouldn't come to this, but the gods are not smiling upon us. We don't have time to debate." Finn held his bag open to show Ivar what he had with him. "I assure you I have thought this through. I will be fine. I brought supplies. I have Earth cash money papers, dried meat, clothes—"

"Unacceptable," Ivar interrupted. "I forbid you from staying."

"You have no authority over me," Finn denied. "You can't forbid me from doing anything. This isn't Var territory."

"And you're not a prince here, dragon," Ivar stated. "You have no protection, no way of calling for help."

"Nobility does not change with location." Finn

did not need the cat-shiftter prince telling him how dangerous his plan was. He well knew of the risk.

"Your royalty is not recognized here." Ivar snatched the bag from Finn's hands and held it tight in his fist. "Get in the portal, or I will throw you in. I will not leave you."

"I left a note explaining this to the king and queen in my room at the palace," Finn tried to explain, but Ivar's determination did not lighten. He was well aware that humans might walk by at any moment. The darkening sky and the enclosed passageway kept them somewhat in the shadows, but the artificial lights illuminated the alleyway enough to see their figures. "Now, go and be well. I'll be here in a year."

Ivar didn't hesitate. He lunged for Finn, grabbing him by his shirt. Finn tried to pull away, and the material ripped.

"You're going home," Ivar commanded. "Get in the portal."

"No." Finn swung his hand to block Ivar's oncoming grip. The force of the contact sent a jolt of pain through his arm.

"Get in the portal." Ivar swung again.

"No." Finn ducked. He tried to angle Ivar so he could push the man through. They struggled for footing, each trying to slam the other toward the portal wall.

Ivar became more aggressive. The glint of his inner cat flashed a bright green in his eyes, threatening to surface. Claws extended from his fingertips. Finn gave a low growl of warning in the back of his throat on instinct. His flesh tingled with the urge to shift, but he knew he couldn't do such a thing on Earth.

"Get in the portal, Finn," Ivar demanded, louder than before.

Finn knew time was running out. The portal could close at any moment. He balled his fist, cocked back his arm, and let fly a punch. It found its mark hitting Ivar flush on the jaw. Finn stumbled as he lost footing on loose debris on the ground.

"Stop," a woman yelled. Her authoritative tone distracted Finn long enough to take his mind off the task which life as he knew it depended upon.

In the shadowed alley, he saw the silhouette of a woman, presumably the one who shouted out to him. She stood, feet shoulder length apart, like it was her turf and they were trespassing.

The unknown woman held up one of the rectangular glowing devices humans seemed to cling to for dear life. It blocked her face from him. Instinctively he walked toward her. "Or I'll call the cops," she threatened.

Finn's attention diverted long enough for Ivar to get the upper hand. The cat-shifter punched him square in the jaw, knocking him senseless before grabbing him by the arm and flinging Finn at the portal like a discarded piece of rubbish.

Finn flailed in the air, his limbs were all over the place. It became impossible to grab onto something solid or find traction of any sort. The familiar pull of portal travel sucked him in, and he became cocooned in a sheath of dense pressure. If he didn't know better, he would have sworn that this was the end.

The air in his lungs became thick, the blood in his veins congealed, and his eyes dried until he could not even cry out from the discomfort. The disassembly process felt like the exact opposite of what really happened. His body was torn into a sextillion pieces, flying like data through the portal tunnel. Their scientists said that the feeling of being compacted was the mind hard at work, willing all the physiological pieces back together once they reached the other side.

The trip was over before he could even fathom that he had failed. Ivar had forced him home. And the fate of his people was being sealed.

4

"STOP!"

Sadie wasn't sure what possessed her to want to break up a street brawl. She'd been thinking of ways to set her blog apart from the many other travel sites. But fighting your way through a dark alley to your next destination might be detrimental to one's health. The men were in her path to scouting out a location to a rumored speakeasy. At her warning shout, the leaner of the two men obeyed, turning to look at her. Her breath caught as the light revealed his face. It was the guy from earlier in the courtyard. His eyes appeared to capture a reflection before the other man grabbed him and shoved him hard into the wall. A bright light flashed, and the man disappeared.

Sadie froze in horror, too petrified by what she witnessed to move. She couldn't even blink.

The remaining man turned on her. That was not a reflection in his glowing eyes. The fur of a tiger sprouted over his face. And then sharp fangs extended from his mouth.

Finally, she screamed as she sprang into action. But alas it was too late. The morphing catlike creature was too fast.

He had a hairy hand over her mouth and had her back against his chest before she took two steps. His sharp nails grazed her skin like carving knives as he dragged her deeper into the alleyway.

Sadie wanted to break free, but his hold was too tight. She kicked her legs, trying to find a foothold on the walls. All she managed to do was cause him to stumble a few times.

"I'm sorry, but this secret can't be revealed," a gruff voice whispered in her ear. She threw an elbow back, making contact with his ribs. The man thrust her forward. She expected to hit the wall but instead felt her body being sucked into a vacuum. At first, the strange feeling didn't hurt. A bright purple light flashed and a loud roar sounded. Then, a stabbing sensation covered her body, reminding her of a junk-yard car being squashed into a block of waste metal.

Sadie cried out in surprise as her muscles seized. She flung forward into the darkness and knocked into someone. The roaring noise abruptly ended as she landed on the mysterious person. She couldn't move right away. The purple light faded, leaving her in pitch black. The way the legs brushed up against her felt like a man. Hard armor covered his chest and thighs. He moaned as if dazed by the fall.

Sadie's arms shook as she pushed off him, and whispered, "Mister?"

He moaned again. Not knowing what else to do, she reached for where his face would be in the dark. Her fingers met with a strange mask. A ridge formed along the bridge of his nose and brow, like touching the hard-plated skin of an alligator. Sadie made a weak noise as she fearfully jerked her hand back.

A furry creature and now this? Logic told her to run, and she had no reason not to listen.

She felt around the stone floor. Her eyes adjusted to the dark, and she detected a soft glow. She crawled past the man on her hands and knees, doing her best not to touch him as she found hold on the rocky surface. She panted loudly no matter how hard she tried to suppress her heavy breathing. She needed to get out of this basement-cave-whatever-it-was. If she could make it to the city streets, she'd be safe.

She flung her hands to find anything in the dark that might block her way to freedom. The light became brighter, giving context to what her hands found. The black stone looked more natural than manmade. She pushed to her feet and ran toward the front of the cave, bursting out of the opening into what should have been a city street.

"No," Sadie mumbled, shaking her head. This couldn't be right. The expansive valley had no place inside city limits. She rubbed her eyes and temples. The colors weren't right. The sky was tinted green and the grass yellow.

Food poisoning? Had she been drugged? Virtual reality?

Sadie felt sane, but her eyes could not be trusted. The breeze against her skin gave her goosebumps. The sweet scent wafting in the air was unmistakable like spun sugar at a carnival. The sound of wind tickling the grass crashed over the valley in a song. None of these elements were reachable from within a dark alleyway in downtown Oxford, Mississippi.

Yet here she was.

To recalibrate, Sadie turned in a slow circle to summon her bearings. She hated how her limbs shook, but she couldn't stop the wobbling.

Fear had a way of superseding all else,

suspending hope and clouding clear thought. Mustering determination from heaven knows where, Sadie made a promise to herself, "I will get through this. Whatever this is."

Whenever things got out of hand or when the going got tough, Sadie promised herself that she would rise above the problem to find the solution, no matter what. It was a trick her mother had taught her.

The valley stretched into the distance with hints of trees and mountains along the horizon. She'd emerged from beneath a jagged crag. The black stones soaked in light and hid the depths within. Above her, two suns shone in the sky. This was a hallucination of some sort. In time the drugs would wear off. In the interim, she needed all her wits about her, so she wouldn't do anything stupider than she had already done to land herself in this mess.

Sadie whimpered. The feeling of being watched caused a shiver to course over her. That is when she noticed the cool sting of tears rolling over her hot cheeks. This delusion could not be real. If she held still, maybe it would all go away.

A slight movement caught her attention, and she gasped, completing her circle. Men waited beside a rocky protrusion, some partially hidden, all silently watching her like living statues. They dressed like the man she'd seen beaten in the alley.

For the longest moment, they merely stared, gazes combing the landscape for any sign of others, it was as if they couldn't believe that she was there. She understood the feeling. This hardly seemed real. One opened his mouth to speak, but the sound that came out was a strange guttural rambling of cacophonous noise. Sadie shook her head and covered her ears.

The man from town stumbled from the cave, holding his temple. Brown hair hid his expression. When he pulled his hand away from his head, blood marred his fingers. He looked up, and a breeze blew his hair back to reveal that his face was covered with hard brown flesh.

At the sight, the onlookers all turned toward her. Their bodies jerked strangely as they leaned forward. They morphed and changed, flesh becoming a hardened shell, eyes glowing with gold, as they shifted forms to become, what Sadie could only describe as part man, part prehistoric creature. Dragon? Talons extended from their fingertips. Fangs protruded from between their lips. They snarled in warning and inched forward as if awaiting a command to attack.

More of the dragon creatures appeared from behind the rocks.

A scream had erupted from her throat before her body did the only thing she could think to do. She ran. As fast as she could to get away from the insanity. Sadie's heart thumped so loudly she couldn't hear what was behind her, but she was sure the dragon men were hunting her. And, once they caught her, she'd surely be dead.

5

FINN TILTED his head and watched the screaming human woman take off across the valley. Turning toward the shifted guards, he frowned and gestured at them to be quiet. "I hit my head in the cave. There is nothing to be alarmed about. We are not under attack by humans. Prince Ivar is by the portal. Go see if he needs help."

The screaming stopped. He glanced over to see the woman had tripped. She pushed up from amongst the tall valley grasses, and the screaming resumed as she ran aimlessly, stumbling as she went. The valley was extensive and it wasn't like she'd reach the forest anytime soon at the pace she was going.

Finn glanced at his fingers. They were bloody

from the wound on his head, but nothing to be worried about. He'd suffered worse. Eventually, the pain would subside.

The screaming continued. He thought about giving chase, but the truth was he felt a little wobbly on his feet. So, instead, he crossed his arms over his chest and waited to see what would happen.

The woman tripped again, and the screaming stopped. She didn't immediately stand.

Finn dropped his arms and took a few steps toward her.

She'd made it a fair distance, but he could sprint to her if he so wanted. Slowly, she pushed up to sitting and jerked her arms up, twisting one way and then the other as if warding off an attack. He stopped and narrowed his eyes, using the power of his shifted sight to see her more clearly. Light brown hair blew past her face, masking her mouth and nose. Brown eyes searched over the valley as if surprised she wasn't being followed. Her arms dropped.

The beauty of the woman took him by surprise. He'd caught a glimpse of her in the alleyway, but not enough to register the full extent of her. It had been hard to concentrate with Ivar's fists coming at him.

Delicate fingers lifted to pull the hair from her face. Her parted lips drew in hard, heavy breaths. For the longest moment, she sat, panting for air, shading her eyes as she peered over the valley in his direction. She didn't appear to see him, not as he saw her. Her lips moved, but he couldn't determine what she was saying.

"We dispatched four guards down the tunnels toward the palace to track the prince," Cleve announced. The portal guard was new to his duties, and Finn often found him a little too eager to please. Such was the way with youth. The man was only forty years old. His predecessor had left through the portal taking several Draig men with him. "We will find him."

The tunnels to the portal were dangerous, with damp, slick stones and narrow pathways. They led to a stairwell inside the dragon-shifter palace. The tunnels were rarely used if it could be avoided. Why would Ivar think to go that route instead of through the safer valley entrance?

"My prince, may I ask? Why were you coming through the tunnels?" Cleve inquired. "Has something happened at the palace? Why is the Var prince with you?"

Finn lifted his hand to quiet the guard. The human woman stood and turned in a slow circle. She might be examining her surroundings, but the movement gave Finn a decent view of her body as the breeze pushed against her clothing. She took two steps to the right before turning and moving five steps to the left, only to end up going back to her original place.

"Who is she?" Cleve asked.

Finn again lifted his hand for silence. "I don't know."

As if coming to a decision, she walked back to the cave.

Finn held his breath as his body tightened in anticipation. He enjoyed the moment, watching her as she moved toward him. The sound of rustling feet through the grasses gave music to her slow, almost purposeful progress. His arms and legs felt heavy. His heartbeat quickened. The undeniable attraction, the surge of excitement, the physical pull, the urge inside his stomach to lunge forward and sweep her into his arms, could this be what men described when they spoke of finding their mate?

When she'd made it within talking distance, she stopped. "Where am I?"

Her question was louder than necessary.

Such a pretty voice, Finn thought.

"Northern mountains," Cleve answered for him, using the Earth language.

Finn frowned at the interruption to his growing fantasy and turned to look at the man. "See to Prince Ivar."

The guard nodded, and it was then, seeing the disappointment at being sent away in the man's expression, that Finn realized he wasn't the only one captivated by this woman.

It would seem the fascination he felt wasn't uniquely his. Cleve was enamored as well. Finn's attraction was strong, so strong it had almost tricked him into believing the feeling was special. But why wouldn't it be strong? She was beautiful. Her skin was soft, her lips attractive and...

"Why am I here?" She stiffened, as if ready to run again. "Why are you looking at me like that?"

Finn wasn't sure how to answer.

"Maybe I should find that other guy. He speaks my language." She stepped to the side, making a wide arc around him toward the cave entrance.

"I speak your language," Finn said. Hopefully this time the beautiful woman would hear him.

"Then tell me why I am here." Panic filled her voice.

"Because you walked here," he gestured behind her, "from there."

"Where is here? And don't say Northern Mountains. North of where? More importantly, *how* did I get here?" Her breathing quickened, and her tone became all the more frantic. "A minute ago, I was in Oxford walking down Faulkner Alley, looking for a hole-in-the-wall place that serves grilled cheese sand-wiches so I could do a write up of it—those stories can sometimes go viral if done right, you know, and I could always use more web traffic—and anyway, now I'm..." She gestured wildly around her. "I'm in the mountains hallucinating. The grass is yellow. The sky is green. Your eyes are glowing. You and those other men are some kind of reptilian-dragon-alliga-tor-whatever."

"We are Draig, we're dragon-shifters," Finn corrected.

"Oh, so the hallucinations are auditory, too. That's good to know." She had given a humorless, nervous laugh before she fidgeted with her fingers.

"It feels like the mountains, I guess. The air is thinner. And I'm having a hard time catching my breath. And I am seeing double." She pointed to the sky. "Am I wrong, or are there two suns?"

"Three," he stated. "The blue one is hidden."

"Of course, it is," she mumbled to herself.

"If you are upset about being here, why did you follow me into the portal?" Finn asked.

"Portal? You mean that bright light? I was pushed against what I thought was a wall by that furry man who threw me into the light." She eyed Finn, waiting for confirmation or any sign that he might be lying to her.

"So, it is the will of the gods, then." Finn nodded. "That is why you are here. You were meant to come." He thought about the guard he'd sent away, and remembered the way he'd looked at this woman. Jealousy filled him to think that she was meant for another. Yet who was he to get in the way if Cleve was her future?

Gudmund, another of the portal guards, appeared. "My prince, I have sent Gale and Cedar —"

The woman gasped at the sudden intrusion and stumbled backward. Gudmund frowned at the interruption. Finn imagined, after hearing Earthmen speak, that Gudmund's voice would sound brusque to the human ear.

"Use the Earth language. She startles easily," Finn ordered. His head throbbed where he'd bumped it, and he absently rubbed near the wound.

"Cleve found satchels in the cave, but Prince Ivar is not there. Are you sure the prince followed you into the tunnels?" Gudmund asked.

Finn turned toward the cave, willing Ivar to appear. "What do you mean Prince Ivar is not there? That's not possible."

"All we found are these items." Gudmund motioned his hand toward the cave and Cleve came out carrying two bags. Finn recognized the satchel as his. It had all the Earth money. "Has a trip been scheduled for tonight?"

Cleve held up the larger black one. "This one is marked with the word, *Saddle*." He lowered it, and it bumped against the rock face.

"It says my name, *Sadie*. And take it easy. It has my laptop inside. You can't bang it around like that." Sadie reached for her satchel. She appeared to get over her fear of them long enough to approach Cleve and snatch her property from him. She took it with her several feet away before digging inside. "Where's my phone? I..." Her expression fell, and she stopped looking. "I was carrying it in the alleyway when that hairy man attacked me. I bet I dropped it. Dammit."

"Hairy man?" Gudmund asked. "Does she mean Prince Ivar? Did you come from the portal? I was not told there was to be travel. The charts say last night's location is not advisable. This valley entrance was locked. I opened it this morning as instructed to let air flow through the caves before the elders come for a tour. We have not neglected our duty."

Finn didn't answer as he hurried into the cave. He knew the gate to the valley had been locked because he'd locked it behind him after they snuck in. "Check the portal! Is it still open? Prince Ivar is on the other side."

Finn ran toward the portal. Someone had lit torches and placed them along the wall. He had known before he reached the doorway that it was too late. The purple light signifying the portal was open had long faded. Carvings of dragons and cats pointed at him to go back to the valley, a symbol of their exodus from Earth, a warning not to return.

That didn't stop him from trying to jump between the statutes to the other side. He fell through the air, not going anywhere but to the back of the cave. The door to the Earth city had closed and couldn't be reopened to that location for another year. Ivar was trapped. Finn's eyes moved to the guard holding his bag full of Earth supplies. The cat-shifting prince had no means to support himself. He was stranded on Earth alone and without means.

"Prince Finn?" Gudmund inquired. "What happened to the Var prince?"

Finn shook his head, too shocked to consider his answer as he whispered, "I don't know."

"The Var King and Queen will not accept this answer," Gudmund warned. "You must return to the palace and pretend that you were never here. If they suspect something happened to their son on Draig watch..."

"I have nothing to hide," Finn denied.

"You have blood trickling down your back from your head, and the cat-shifter prince is missing. It does not look good," Gudmund insisted. Finn knew the man was worried about losing a prince while he was on guard duty. It was a valid concern. With the fate of the portal already in contention, people were already upset. It was one thing to stay behind willingly. Quite another to get locked out when no one knew you were going in the first place.

Finn's eyes moved toward Sadie. She'd followed them inside and was watching their every move.

"The men will remain quiet about your presence here. I will make sure of it. She is the only witness. How should we deal with her?" the guard asked in their native Draig tongue so the woman couldn't understand.

Finn considered his options. Shove her through the portal as soon as it reopened and hope that the

Earth authorities wherever she landed thought she was crazy when she tried to tell them what had happened to her? Talk to her and make her understand the severity of the situation? He knew nothing about this woman except that she was attractive and had a lovely voice, and her eyes held him locked in a return gaze.

"Will someone please explain what's happening?" the woman asked.

"Prince Finn?" the Draig guard insisted, still speaking the shifter language. "Do you want us to make her disappear? I have cousins who live in Mining Camp."

"That place is nothing but tents and miners." Finn frowned. It was no place for a woman to go.

"They will not care if she is a true mate. They will take her and—"

"Mine," Finn stated before his plan was fully formed. Ivar was gone. Though not as Finn intended, the cat-shifter's disappearance would keep the portal open for another year. That left it up to Finn to go through with the other plan. He would take a mate, any mate, and make the relationship work by any means necessary. "You will do nothing. She's mine."

6

Did the handsome man just announce that she belonged to him?

Sadie stepped back to allow for space so she could fully assess the statement. For good measure, she looked around, checking that there wasn't another *"she"*. Maybe it was the sheer audacity of the guy or the shock she was in from all that had happened, but only part of her wanted to correct him, while the idea resonated inside her more than she cared to admit.

Some of their accents were difficult to understand, but she was pretty sure one kept saying, "prince," and they both looked extremely worried about something.

Their eyes narrowed as they studied her. Why were they looking at her like that?

"I won't say anything," Sadie whispered. "I don't know anything to say."

"Fetch the tent," the one called Finn ordered. "And the king and queen."

"What's the tent?" Sadie tried to back out of the cave. She pressed tightly to the side as the guard hurried past her toward the valley. She should have kept running the first time instead of coming back. Surely there was a town or a road or an... astronaut to explain why she saw two suns.

"I am sure you have many questions, but here is what you need to know. You're on the planet of Qurilixen. I am what your people call a dragon-shifter. You came through the portal from Earth. I know this will be challenging to understand, but this is your new reality. I apologize that you were not given a choice, but I will not question the will of the gods. You are meant to be here, and your sacrifice will not go unnoticed. You will be saving a great many people."

Sacrifice? Am I to be sacrificed? What the hell kind of nightmare is this?

Sadie glanced to what looked to be a doorway. That had to be the way she'd come through. She remembered crawling out of a cave, but not this one, which meant she'd somehow been transported here. Her daddy didn't raise a coward. It was now or never.

Sadie dashed forward, running toward the portal to escape. Her heart pounded, sending adrenaline through her veins to power her movement. Finn blinked in confusion, lifting his hands.

She leaped past him in the general direction of the portal. As she felt her body become airborne, she waited for the purple light that would take her home.

All that came was darkness.

FINN CAUGHT the woman as her body dropped to the floor. Out of all his travels to Earth, he'd never met a human as strange as this one. She seemed to enjoy screaming and running. Only this time she ran straight into a wall.

He lowered her gently to the cave floor and held her against his chest. Her soft breath caressed his chin. For a moment, the intimate sensation stunned him. Again, he held his breath. The torchlight flickered over her features, revealing the red mark on her cheek and forehead where she'd hit the stone. Worry filled him. He wasn't sure what to do about the injury, so he kept her in his arms and willed her to open her eyes. "Sadie?"

Long hair spilled over his arm, creating lines that flowed over his flesh like contours on a map. His gaze followed the trails of hair toward her mouth. The sound of her breathing created a hypnotic rhythm that mesmerized him. This felt like something, but how could he be sure?

Dragons were supposed to know—one look, one second, and he would have known if she were his *forever*.

But he'd seen her in the alleyway, watched her run in the valley, saw the infatuated way Cleve stared at her. How could he know if the attraction he felt was the real thing or the lust of a lonely man?

Dragons were not supposed to doubt themselves when it came to a mate.

Everyone said the gods spoke to them in that perfect moment—a strong force that hit them and made them speechless—astonishing them under the sheer force of emotion for the rest of their lives.

The only thing that had hit Finn was Ivar's fist, then the cave floor.

Even now the back of his skull throbbed with a dull pain.

"I may not be your true mate," Finn whispered to

the woman, knowing this would be the only time he'd admit the words out loud. It broke his heart a little because he so wanted her to be his in all ways. "But I promise I will make you a fine husband. I will be dedicated and faithful and kind. You will never go without. You will be a princess and given the love of my people. All I have to offer you will be yours. I must believe the gods put you in my path for a reason. We are meant to secure the future of shifters, both cat and dragon. I suppose they wish to know we are willing to sacrifice."

She made a small noise but did not wake up.

"We must keep the portals open. My people will die out, Sadie. Please understand why we must do this. When we came to this planet, we were punished for reasons I don't understand, and female shifters stopped being born. People tried to have more children to make up for the fact, but the majority of those babies have been male. Our scholars say we will die out completely within two generations if something is not done. I tell you this to explain why I must take you to the tent and why there is not more time to decide."

"Dream... over," she mumbled.

He didn't know what she meant, but the words made sense to him. "Yes. The dream is over."

"My prince," Gudmund appeared. "I sent a request to the palace to do as you commanded. The marriage tent will take some time. It is in storage."

"Any tent will do," Finn said. "I need nothing fancy, just fast."

"As you wish. I will have the men erect one immediately." Gudmund began to leave, only to stop. "And perhaps a medic for your bride?"

Finn nodded, ashamed that he hadn't thought of it. He had a hard time concentrating. "Yes. And a medic. She hit her head."

Gudmund frowned. "And perhaps a medic for you as well, my prince."

Finn touched the dried blood in his hair. "Yes. For me as well."

7

SADIE GASPED, flinging her arms as she came out of the strange dream. She jerked in disorientation before laughing softly at herself. The hotel room was dark. It was night. It was strange that no light came through the seam in the curtains. Normally street-lights intruded like a nightlight.

She blinked, straining her hearing. She detected rustling inside the darkness, and someone breathing.

The comfort of peacefulness quickly spiraled into a stark pitch darkness in which Sadie imagined ghoulish creatures. Lurking, waiting, ready to pounce at any movement that she made.

What should have been a soft mattress felt like a thin blanket carelessly tossed on the rocky ground. A tear escaped and slid over her cheek at the thought of how helpless she was. This nightmarish reality defied all logic. This couldn't be happening.

This couldn't be.

"This can't be happening," she whispered into the abyss, not filtering her panic.

But then something did happen, reversing the fear that had risen out of the darkness.

A hand moved over her stomach in an intimate caress as if to hold her. Sadie tried letting go of her anxiety. She needed her sanity if she was to get through whatever this was.

There was warmth and safety in the touch, but also familiarity. This was a new sensation for Sadie, and seemed foreign and out of place in her life. The hand rested, falling still. She held her breath and leaned to enable the caress as she exhaled. The hand moved with each intake of air, and turned the simple act of breathing into something complex, even sensual.

Part of her didn't want to move, afraid that what was happening would end, or turn out to be something sinister by someone unsavory. But, then her mind moved past the sensory qualities of someone's touch, evil or not—which her body obviously yearned for—to the rocks poking her in the back. Half-heartedly Sadie pulled the hand off her.

A gruff noise sounded, a succession of indecipherable foreign words. The loud voice was out of place in the quiet.

A bright light shone through the curtains. No, not curtains. A tent flap. She lifted her hand to block the sudden intrusion from her eyes. A figure loomed over her in the small space.

Seeing her, the man's language changed. "Who do we have in here?"

She spread her fingers to see his face. Age marked the man's features in tiny lines. Shadows made the wrinkles more pronounced. There was something cold within that gaze, removed from the situation, no warmth, no welcoming smile, no curiosity.

"I see." The man sighed loudly, and then commanded, "Come out of there. This is no place for royalty."

The flap closed, but Sadie was wide awake, and the now opened tent did little to block daylight.

Sadie turned to see Finn lying next to her. His eyes were closed. She touched his chest.

"Finn? Who was that?" Sadie asked as if what was happening was part of her everyday life.

When Finn didn't answer, Sadie decided she was too tired to come up with an alternative to the reality someone had gone to a lot of trouble to create. She'd heard of cosplay and historical reenactments, but this was on another level.

Three suns, green sky? she thought. *This is the work of a megalomaniac who is both delusional and color blind.*

Squaring her shoulders, Sadie decided she'd give it her best shot and try to turn the situation around somehow to her advantage. Clearing her throat, "Finn? That man wants us to follow him."

She tried shaking him, but his body moved like it was a lump of lead.

"I don't know what to do." Sadie took several deep breaths before she could force herself to open the tent flap.

The light hit Finn's face. A pale undertone added sickness to his features. His chest lifted as he breathed.

"Finn?"

He didn't answer.

"Finn?" She gave him a small shake. Still, no answer. "I'll find you help."

The tent hung low to the ground, affixed to an outcropping of rocks. The sagging walls hardly looked weather-worthy, as if someone had hurriedly strung up a blanket to make shade. A couple of blankets covered the hard ground, providing little padding.

"Come out," a woman said.

So far she'd seen only men in this place, and the idea of another woman gave her some measure of comfort. Sadie crawled from the tent only to find a dress blocking her way. Her eyes traveled upward. The lavender folds of the thick skirt belonged as the centerpiece at a Renaissance Faire, the cream under-dress peeking through the bodice and along the arms. Tiny dragons were embroidered over the neckline, stiffening the material so that it lifted and held firmly in place.

Even if she were truly only an actress, the woman carried herself like a noblewoman. The disapproval in her expression was not hidden as she looked down at Sadie. A delicate hand reached forward as the woman motioned Sadie to stand.

Sadie scrambled to her feet, drawn to obey the woman's voice. She motioned to the sick man in the tent. "I thin—"

"Welcome to the family of Draig, Lady..." The woman's eyes narrowed as if upset by something, but she continued, "my lady. I wish you much happiness and a blessed marriage."

"Thank you—wait, marriage?" Sadie questioned. "Listen, this guy in the tent is—"

"I am Queen Galina. This is my husband, King Severin." The queen gestured to the man next to her. His clothes matched in their regal appearance with soft fabrics and embroidered hems, just as his expression matched the stress on his wife's face.

"I think there is a mistake. I'm not an actress," Sadie whispered. "I don't know what part it is I'm meant to play."

The king and queen glanced at each other, bemused somewhat.

"Where is my son?" The king questioned, only to call, "Finn? Step out of the tent."

Sadie looked over her shoulder. "I've been trying to tell you. He's not well. Please, call an ambulance. He needs a doctor."

Her words caused a flurry of movement. The queen pushed past her to look inside the tent. With a hard jerk, the king tore the blanket from its anchors, tossing the material aside. Sadie was pushed back as men gathered forward to look at the unconscious prince on the ground.

"Send for a medic," the scary man, who'd first stuck his head into the tent, ordered. He was the only one not pushing forward to inspect the prince. When she stumbled near him, he reached out and grabbed her upper arm. He held her tight. His disapproving frown seemed almost sinister, but in truth everything about this day was tainted by fear.

Sadie tried to pull her arm, but his grip tightened.

"Stay where you are, my lady," the man said. "We cannot have the new princess traipsing over the countryside looking like..." His eyes dipped over her with disgust. "Like a human. This situation is degrading enough."

"I'm not a princess," Sadie denied.

"On that we agree," the man quipped.

"So what are you? Like the king's bodyguard?" Sadie returned the man's frown. The hold on her arm remained firm, but he stopped squeezing when she stopped trying to pull free.

"I am Lord Montague," he said. "Head of the elder council."

"Lord Montague? Is that like being a member of some Shakespearian parliament?" Sadie mocked. "Let me guess. He's Romeo? I'm Juliet? And I just fucked up the death scene?"

"Stop talking," Montague commanded. "Your words have no meaning here."

The chaos of the encampment drew her attention. Two men carried Finn from the tent to a softer patch of tall yellow grasses. Gudmund said something she couldn't understand and pointed toward the trees. Two of the creatures who were shifted into dragon form ran toward them. Sadie stiffened and tried to pull away.

Montague grunted. "It is only the runner bringing the medic."

"I don't understand what I'm doing here," Sadie mumbled, unable to take her eyes off the alien faces.

"All you need to do is stand there and be quiet. Do you think you can manage that much?" Montague's condescending tone wasn't appreciated, but she nodded her head in understanding. Maybe he was worried about Finn. That would explain his attitude. Or, maybe he was just an asshole.

Sadie glanced at the sky, seeing a blue sun with the two yellow. It served as a reminder that she wasn't anywhere close to home. The only ally she seemed to have in this place was unconscious. Too many thoughts whirled in her mind that she had a hard time concentrating.

Why did the queen say she was married? She wasn't even dating. Why was she hidden in a tent? Why did her forehead ache? How could she convince the man holding her arm to let her go? Three suns. New planet. Dragon men. Romeo

Montague. Not a good omen, that. Romeo and Juliet both died tragically and stupidly. But she was too old to be Juliet. Wasn't Juliet like sixteen or something? Thirteen? No, that didn't sound right. This felt like something she should remember from High School English. Wait, why was she thinking of High School English?

"The queen asked you a question." Montague gave her a small shake.

"I don't know the answer." Sadie rushed. She had been a little too preoccupied with her oncoming panic attack that she hadn't heard the question. She met the queen's gaze.

"You don't know how you came to be here?" the queen asked, arching a brow.

"Oh, that. A fuzzy man was fighting with Finn." Sadie waited to see what their reaction would be. Maybe, the head prankster would call "cut" now that she had made a complete fool of herself. Still, there was nothing but humorless expressions on stone cold faces.

Clearing her throat, Sadie decided it was time to throw-down the ace up her sleeve. "He threw me into a *portal*, the furry man, not Finn." Sadie glanced from Montague to the queen. Maybe now they'd admit to the hidden camera? But there was no such luck. Instead, they appeared to want more. "And I flew through the portal. I thought it was the black door with the skull, but now I'm sure it was the wall." Still, they looked at her. She didn't know what they expected her to say. "And I landed on this side of the *portal*." Once again, exaggerating the weirdest most absurd idea that ever left her lips.

The queen motioned some nearby guards to move away to give them privacy.

"Fuzzy man? Do you mean Prince Ivar?" Montague prompted.

Sadie shrugged, not liking their attention focused so fully on her. "If that's what you call the cat-man in the alley. One moment he was human and the next he was, he had fur, he..." Her voice trailed off, not sure of what the politically correct way to explain *became a scary hairball*.

"Ivar and Finn were fighting?" Montague said to the queen. The question sounded rhetorical.

"No. That is not possible. They have been friends since childhood," Queen Galina dismissed. "They know better than to make a scene. Besides, Ivar would never go on an unsanctioned trip through the portal."

Montague grunted and glanced to where Finn's body was blocked by the medic. It was clear they both knew Finn well and they apparently believed he could make an unsanctioned trip through the portal. The man evidently had a penchant for going against the grain.

"How is Finn?" Sadie leaned, trying to see.

"What were they fighting about?" The queen lifted her arms over her chest. "You?"

"What? Me? No. I don't know. I don't speak the language. They were yelling. I tried to break up the fight, but then... Ivar?" They both nodded when she paused. "Finn hit Ivar. Ivar hit Finn. Finn fell through the wall. Then Ivar grabbed me and pushed me in. I'm sorry, but that's all I know."

Montague mumbled something under his breath that Sadie couldn't understand.

"It could have been any number of things," the queen answered Montague, partly in defense. "Speak the Earth language. The men will hear you. Most of them have not taken Earth lessons and know very few words."

"The princes broke protocol by going through the portal," Montague said. "Prince Finn willfully, and not for the first time, disobeyed the will of the elders."

"It was not a direct order," the queen defended her son. "We had only set a meeting to discuss closing the portals. No decree was set forth saying no one was to travel through them."

"It was implied," Montague argued.

"It seems much is being implied by you, my lord." The queen's expression stayed calm, but her eyes flashed with an inner glow.

Sadie didn't want to be in the middle of their power play. "Seriously, is Finn going to be all right? He didn't look that great."

"Of course, you're worried about your husband." Montague loosened his hold on her arm. Sadie yanked away from him. She kept a wary eye on the irritated queen and grumpy lord.

Making an arc, Sadie moved around the dragon men watching over Finn, until she spotted an opening and squeezed through it.

He lay on his back, blinking slowly. A low groan left him as he turned to look at her. Their eyes met, and she felt a deep sense of relief in knowing he was awake.

None of this made logical sense, but it was time for Sadie to remember who she was. She was resilient. She was good in new situations, and at making friends. She was observant. She was strong. She could handle herself.

Against dragons?

Sadie closed her eyes and took a deep breath. *Yes. I can handle myself against dragons.*

"What kind of princess agrees to be married under an old blanket?" Montague muttered under his breath as he passed by. "Finn has brought disgrace yet again to the royal family."

Sadie turned and locked eyes with the man, letting him know she'd heard him. His eyes flashed with yellow as if daring her to contradict him. She looked away.

"Lord Montague has always been ill-tempered," the queen said, coming to her side. "But he is not wrong. This marriage ceremony was not well done." The woman placed a hand lightly on Sadie's arm, smiling prettily. The expression did not meet her eyes. "You are to say nothing. Do not speak. Do not hint. Do not answer questions with so much as a nod. Do you understand?"

Sadie stared at the woman and didn't move.

"Good," Queen Galina acknowledged the non-answer. "Now try to smile. Stop looking as if Finn is at death's door and that you doubt the gods meant for your marriage to last a long time. My son is strong. He will not die from a little bump on the head."

Sadie tried, but she was sure the pathetic attempt

at pleasantness was completely lost in what had to be a psychotic expression.

"I was told the princess also required my services for her head?" the medic approached the queen. His words were stunted as if the language was difficult for him to pronounce. He eyed Sadie's strange smile and kept his distance.

"Do you require a medic?" the queen asked. Sadie dropped the crazy expression and didn't answer. The queen gave her a once over and then dismissed the medic in their native tongue.

Finn stood and said something to make those around him laugh. He wobbled a little on his feet as he moved toward her.

Sadie glanced at the queen before defying the order not to speak. "Are you well?"

Finn gave her an easy smile. "Rough landing. I was just telling them there is a reason our dragon doesn't fly."

The queen made a small sound.

"I guess that's partially my fault since I was the one who landed on you." She didn't expect the round of laughter that followed her statement, and couldn't help a nervous laugh. "So, I think I might have hit my head as well. Everyone keeps saying that we're married?"

Finn's eyes narrowed as he glanced at his parents. "I'm assuming the queen has welcomed you to the family?"

"Yes." Sadie nodded.

"Then don't worry about it, *fea*, all is taken care of," Finn said.

Sadie narrowed her brow in confusion. "What is taken care of?"

"The ceremony," he answered.

"But—"

"You must be tired, my dear," the queen interrupted. "Finn, take the lady by the back way to the palace."

"The tunnels?" he questioned, furrowing his brow. "But—"

"It will give you some privacy." The queen gave another of her overly studied smiles. "The king and I will see you at the palace."

Finn nodded and offered his arm to Sadie. She took it only because she wasn't sure what else to do. Getting away from the crowd seemed like a good idea. Finn strolled as if they had nowhere to be. As the men watched them, she saw flashes of gold cross several of their eyes. Some even acted as if they would shift as brown patches molded their cheeks and foreheads into hard armor, but they held their humanoid forms.

She glanced at Finn, and his eyes also glinted with an inner light. For some reason she couldn't explain, the reminder of the dragon floating just beneath his surface didn't frighten her. His abilities and strength could easily overtake her, but then so could any human bodybuilder. So why should a little dragon genetics worry her? Sadie knew how to read people upon first meetings, and these dragon men acted human enough for her to get some sense of them. Everything Finn did when he was around her was gentle. He moved with grace, keeping his arm loose as she held it. She didn't detect aggression in him. There was a stiffness to his shoulders as if he carried a great invisible burden.

When they reached the inside of the cave, he dropped her arm and leaned against the rock wall. He took a deep breath and held his head. "I need a moment."

"I knew it. You need a doctor." Sadie motioned to the portal statues. "Turn that door thing on and let's find a hospital."

"It doesn't work like that. The portal won't take you back to that village if that is what you are thinking. It only opens during certain times and the next opening isn't safe for passage." Finn lifted a hand toward her shoulder. "Let me carry that bag for you."

Sadie shook her head denying him the opportunity to help her. "I've got it. She said as she was already questioning her motives for not letting him be a gentleman to her. Maybe she thought that she'd owe Finn something in return for the kind gesture. Maybe she was practicing her independence as a strong woman. Or, was it because she didn't trust him?

The moment lingered a little longer than it should. Whatever the truth was, Sadie had maintained control by the simple act of saying no.

Finn nodded and instead reached for a torch. He led the way past the portal into a dark tunnel. "Watch where you step and let me know if I walk too fast."

Sadie frowned, disguising what she thought as she promised herself that she should memorize her way back to the portal. Eventually, she would have to go home. Walking too fast wasn't a problem. Finn made slow progress. Then again, memorizing a path wasn't an issue either. There was only one direction forward.

In some ways, this felt like an archeological expedition—meeting royalty of some remote tribe no one in the United States knew about. Too bad she couldn't do a write up on their food. No one on Earth would believe she'd gone to... "Where are we again? What do you call your planet?"

"Qurilixen," Finn answered.

No one would believe she'd gone to the planet of Qurilixen. Oh, but imagine the website hits and advertising fees if they did. She'd often daydreamed about going abroad to work, but so far, her site only covered travel in America. Competition was fierce, and she needed to keep her content fresh to keep her site relevant. For a moment, Sadie let her mind stray further than it was safe to do under the circumstances as she wondered if there was internet connection here on planet Qurilixen.

Probably not.

"Not much farther." The words so low she wasn't sure if he said them to reassure himself or her. When the torch swayed, she took it from him. The smoke curled from the tip of the torch further contaminating already stale air.

"What will happen?" Sadie studied the orange light reflecting off his back. It outlined his hair and broad shoulders, giving her something to focus on in the dark.

"We're going to the palace. I need to rest," he said.

"And after that?"

"We'll eat."

"And after that?" she insisted.

"I'll show you around the palace if you like and introduce you to everyone."

"Then what?"

"I suppose then I'll introduce you to Princess Eve. She is married to my brother, Kyran, and is from Earth as well. She has been instrumental in teaching us about your culture and has expanded our knowledge of your language."

None of these were the answer she was seeking. She wanted to know what would happen tomorrow, and the next day, next week. And ultimately when she could go home. "And, after these meet-and-greets, what happens?"

He made a small noise and rubbed the back of his head. "I don't know. I don't plan my schedule in such detail. Prince Ivar's family will require delicate handling, and I'm sure I'll have to speak to the council of elders at some point."

"Lord Montague?" Sadie wrinkled her nose. She imagined she could still feel his grip on her arm. "Good luck. That one's a real peach."

"Don't take anything that man says personally. He never married, and I'm convinced the loneliness has made him surly." Finn bumped his hip into a small outcropping of rock. "Ow. Careful."

Sadie adjusted the torchlight and stepped around the protrusion.

"Lord Montague has not liked me since I was a child. He thinks I'm frivolous with my time and..." Finn sighed. "I should not be saying this."

"And?" Sadie prompted, wanting to hear the rest.

Finn stopped walking and turned toward her. The firelight outlined his features, caressing his cheek and neck, bordering his lips and casting shadows under his chin. Finn took the torch and jammed the handle into a crack in the rock.

When he resumed his place before her, the distorted light struck in such a way that his mouth was perfectly illuminated, drawing her focus to his lips.

"What do you wish to know?" he asked.

It took her a moment to register his words. "What were you going to say? Why doesn't Montague like you?"

"I'm not sure he likes anyone," Finn admitted. "When I was a boy, my brother and I, we were sent to this encampment near Crystal Lake. Lord

Montague was put in charge, a task he did not appreciate since he does not have a fondness for children. To be fair, children do not have a fondness for him either." Finn paused and tilted his head. She watched his alluring lips lift into a smile. "Anyway, I convinced several of the others to sneak away for a night swim. We were trying to grab crystals on the bottom of the lake. I was the first in and the last out."

"He holds a grudge because you broke curfew and went for a swim when you were a boy?" Sadie arched a brow. "That hardly seems reasonable."

"I wasn't exactly breathing when I came out," Finn said. "I hit my head on a rock. A couple of the other boys pulled me from the water, and a guard revived me. I did manage to get the only crystal that night. It made me a hero to the other boys. However, word spread and Montague was humiliated that a dragon prince almost died on his watch. It didn't help that I told the story to anyone who would listen and started wearing the crystal around my neck. I thought it was... I'm not sure of the right word, but very worthy of bragging about. Montague probably thought I was purposefully taunting him with it. Maybe I was. He has often scolded me for not taking my royal position seriously, or him, for that mattress."

"I think you mean matter," Sadie said. "His position for that matter. Mattress is what you sleep on. For that matter is an expression."

"Is it not a bed on which one sleeps?"

"A mattress is part of a bed." Sadie felt her breathing deepen. It sounded overly loud in the tunnels.

"For that *madder*?" Finn shook his head. "I think you are wrong. I do not think anger comes to play in this. He is ill-tempered, but I do not think he has rage."

"If I had to guess, I'd say he was a narcissist who is used to being in power. I've come across a few like him in my time," Sadie said, thinking of some of the people her father had worked with over the years.

"I don't know what a narcissist is, but I do know he likes his position in the council of elders." Finn lifted a hand to touch her cheek. "Have I answered your question? I do not wish to speak about Lord Montague, and I doubt you wish to either."

"Oh?" Sadie didn't want the caress to stop. She gravitated closer to him.

"Why haven't you asked me about our marriage? I would think you'd have questions."

When she looked at him, she didn't feel fear. She felt safe. That didn't mean she accepted what he said at face value. "Because I never agreed to be married.

It's not recognized on my," she stuttered a little before managing, "my pl-planet. It won't affect my taxes. I'm not dating, so it doesn't have an impact on any current relationship status. And, frankly, I have bigger concerns."

"But finding people to share in your life is what living is all about—family, friends, a wife." The caress over her cheek was soft enough to cause shivers. "Otherwise, why do we do anything? What bigger concern can there be than finding your mate?"

His romantic notion was sweet, but life wasn't just about *sweet*. "For one, I'm on an alien planet. Two, I have no way of meeting my work deadlines if I'm here. If I don't work, I don't eat. Literally. Three, I lost my phone and have no way of calling my mother. Four, I—"

Warm lips found hers cutting off her words. The intimacy took her by surprise. She gasped, standing wide-eyed and rigid as his lips moved against hers. Finn's tongue brushed her mouth but did not seek entrance. Every thought and worry seemed to melt away, not holding meaning in this dark tunnel filled with firelight.

First meets are easy.

Sadie trusted her instincts and was not scared of the attraction she felt. Her lips began to move, mimicking his kiss before searching for more. She gave a light moan and leaned into him. It was his turn to act surprised. His body tensed as her hands moved up his chest to land on his shoulders.

"I'm sorry I didn't give you a choice," he whispered against her mouth.

"Ivar is the one who shoved me through the portal. I don't blame you for that. I'm the one who interfered with your fight," she answered. The evidence of his attraction was all too apparent as it pressed against her stomach. When she tried to resume the kiss, he gently pushed her back. Sadie blinked in confusion, glancing down the tunnel to see what would cause him to stop. There was nothing but darkness beyond the torchlight.

Finn took the torch from the wall and again walked before her. "The stairs are close. Come. We can discuss more later."

"Ah, ok?" Sadie touched her lips. What just happened? She'd been ready to take their kiss a step further, and the man stopped her? Sure, the tunnels weren't the most romantic of places, but she didn't see why that would stop him.

8

Finn remembered little about the walk from the tunnels to his bed. Being aroused by Sadie's mere closeness and drowsiness from his head injury combined to play havoc on his barely lucid mind. When the blood had rushed downward from one affliction to the other, the effect was both dizzying and delightful at the same time. Too bad, he'd been so dizzy that he'd been unable to act on his desire for her.

He had vague recollections. At the time, he'd believed that he'd been able to play the part of competent tour guide. But now, lying alone in his bed, he was beginning to doubt his belief, in fact, he suspected that he might've been laughable, even cringe-worthy.

The large dragon banner hung within his view. He knew it was there but had seen the royal insignia so many times his mind ignored it. Finn took the old decoration and what it meant for granted.

The prince's large bed dominated the raised platform. It was as if the carpenter had decided his bed was to be a throne in his room. Everything around him was meant as a reminder of who he was and what was expected—not only to others but to himself. Such was the pressure of prince-hood to be perfect. Though, such reminders probably only served to encourage his rebellious behavior.

The idea of taking stairs to bed seemed unnatural to Finn. There had been many a drunken night where he'd stumbled on his way up. One should fall into a bed and not have to climb stairs to get in.

Finn rolled onto his back, using the movement to test his head. The pain had subsided enough that he could concentrate. Feeling heat, he noticed the fireplace had been lit. The wooden box he kept on the mantel was out of place. With a frown, he rolled over the side, bypassing the stairs as his feet landed on the floor. Crossing the room, he went to open the box. Treasure from childhood filled the inside—a rock roughly shaped like a dragon, the crystal he'd pulled from the bottom of the lake, a piece of round metal imprinted with the Medical Alliance for Planetary Health insignia that he'd received from a visiting dignitary, and other random bits and pieces. He pushed his finger through the memorabilia of his life thus far. The feel of cold steel and earthy rock reminded Finn of who he was and his responsibility to his people. All the trinkets appeared accounted for.

"I hope you don't mind that I lit the fire." Sadie's voice had a certain quality to it, a sincerity that was hard to fake.

Sadie reminded Finn of how he was going to save his people from extinction.

Finn flipped the lid of the treasure box shut. It made a thud, ending his solitary time inside his head, a dangerous pastime in which he could waste hours indulging in hypothetical notions that had little or no consequence on his or his people's future. A smile came to him as he turned to her.

Sadie lay on the couch, out of sight from where he could see from his bed.

"The palace doctor said the medicine he gave you might make you feel a little drowsy," Sadie continued, sitting up. Messy waves of her hair tousled around her shoulders, framing her delicate and refined features. "You've been asleep for a very long time."

Finn stared at her, blinking slowly, as he struggled to form words. Maybe he wasn't as coherent as he first thought. He had a feeling that there was a long list of things he should attend to, but he couldn't remember a single one.

"Sit." She patted the couch.

Finn obeyed. He leaned his head back, letting his eyes roam. They followed the long pull string up to the high vaulted ceiling. The string could draw curtains open and closed on the overhead dome window. By the soft light leaking through a crack in the material, he guessed it was late evening or early morning.

"Are you feeling better?" she asked.

Her gentle fingers moved along his hairline. Closing his eyes, Finn focused his thoughts. "I apologize for not being a better host."

The fingers stopped. "A better host? You were badly injured."

"It's just a bump," he denied. "I'll be fine."

Sadie cupped his cheek, turning his face so he looked at her.

The soft light created a perfect silhouette of her,

adding a softness to the moment that mesmerized him.

"You don't remember what happened, do you? We came up the stairs from the tunnels, and you started wobbling and making strange noises. I couldn't understand what you were saying the entire time. I had to practically drag you to the top. The two guards at the entrance carried you here and sent for a medic. You were knocked around pretty hard by that Ivar character, and my landing on you after coming through the portal didn't help. You kept insisting that Ivar was lost, and it was your fault he didn't... something."

"Didn't make it back," Finn concluded. "Who heard me?"

"Everyone. The guards. The medic. Your parents." Sadie drew her hand away from him and tucked it behind her head as she turned on the couch to study him. Her knee lifted onto the cushioned seat. "Your parents quickly ushered everyone out of here and then posted guards outside the door. The medic came a few times with the queen, and they brought some kind of fruit and a tray with blue bread and meat, but other than that..."

"I am glad they fed you," Finn said. "Did you enjoy the meal?"

"Meals," Sadie corrected.

Finn glanced up at the ceiling as if the shade of light coming through the window would reveal to him the day. It didn't. "How many meals?"

"Finn, you've been out of it for at least two days," Sadie declared. "I can't be sure because apparently, this planet is like towns in places like Northern Alaska and Antarctica that have twenty-four hours of endless daylight. There are guards on the door. I tried to leave once, and they stopped me. We're being held prisoner in here."

"Prisoner?" Finn shook his head in denial. "I'm sure that is not true. The guards were probably trying to look after you, and you misunderstood. Not all have mastered the Earth language. There is no reason why you would be held in anything but the highest esteem by my people."

"I assume you mean English when you say that? Earth has many languages." Sadie wore a plain dress that did not indicate any part of her new station in life. He was a little ashamed of that fact, considering she was his wife and should be given finer things to reflect the responsibilities he was asking her to take on.

"Yes. We have seen this for ourselves. English comes the most natural for us because of our ancestor's time on Earth. The Var do well with your Nordic dialects. Something about their cat voices that make the sound more easily than we do."

"Ancestors?" Sadie prompted. Her eyes lit up, and if she'd been sitting alone in the room, watching him sleep for days, he could well imagine she was starved for conversation. He'd never gone days without talking to someone.

"The Draig and Var ancestors came from Earth many years ago through the portals. We have reopened those portals to travel back to our native homeland."

"Wait, so you're not aliens so much as displaced Earthlings?" Sadie sat up straighter, clearly wanting to know more. "Did the government know? Is this an Area 51 type thing?"

"I have heard Roswell and Mogul speak of that place," Finn answered. "They come as visiting dignitaries who represent the Medical Alliance for Planetary Health. They travel by ship, not portal. When I was a boy, they gave me trinkets from the different universes."

"And what do these aliens look like?" Sadie gave him a skeptical smile.

"They're about this tall." He held his hand about four feet from the floor. "With heads about twice the size of yours. Large, shiny eyes, and tiny holes for a nose. Humanoid shaped bodies, but with longer limbs. Oh, and gray skin. The first time I saw them, I thought they were naked, but they were just wearing these skintight gray jumpsuits. And they talked like this—*click, click-click-click, click-er-click.*"

Sadie threw back her head and laughed. "Good one. You had me going there for a moment. Little gray men. Next, you'll tell me they like to anal probe."

"No. I believe quite the opposite. Prince Rafe, Ivar's brother, told me they stopped going to Earth because humans kept trying to get them to do it."

Sadie laughed harder. "I can see why Lord Monty doesn't think you take things seriously."

"Monty?"

"Montague," she corrected. "Good ole stodgy Monty."

Finn grinned. He doubted Lord Montague would enjoy the nickname. He needed to remember to use it a few times until it became the nobleman's moniker with the people.

"So, why did your people leave Earth to begin with?" Sadie queried. "Oh, wait, are you hungry? I can go beg the prison guards for a crust of bread."

"Why would you go to the dungeons to..." Finn

paused. "Oh, you mean the guards at my door." The prince pushed up, feeling as if his strength and focus was somewhat returning to him.

Feeling better by the second, he went over to the door and opened it as if it were a test of his recovery.

A guard appeared, and Finn conversed with him in their shared language until the prince remembered his new bride.

"Food for my wife and me," he said proudly before closing the door and turning around to face Sadie seated on the couch.

It was like a veil had been lifted as he eyed his prize across the room. Rejoining her on the sofa, he sat close to her. Naturally, he was drawn to her. He felt that it was his mission to make her smile and laugh again. "Monty was one of the elders that came here from Earth as a child. There aren't many of them left, but the way the men tell the story, human culture began to change and form new religions. Before, shifters and dragons, and all manner of magical creatures, lived together in harmony. After these new beliefs had taken hold, humans attacked non-humans. They came in the night with their swords and fire. They claimed we made a pact with some man named Demon though there is no record of this man in our royal library. Our people escaped and caved in the rocks around the portal to keep anyone from going back, and to keep humans from finding their way here."

Sadie's expression fell. "Swords and fire? When you say this happened a few years ago, you mean... the Medieval period? Exactly how hold is Monty?"

"I don't know exactly. At least not in Earth calculations. Your human standards of measurements are not my strong point. Maybe two or three hundred years." Finn let his hand move a little closer to her leg. He remembered a hazy kiss in the tunnels and was confident she'd been returning his embrace before dizziness took hold of him. His fingers tingled as if being pulled closer to her. He tried to resist, reminding himself that she had not come through the portal willingly and that he had not asked her properly to marry him.

"If humans were so bad to you, why did you come back?" she asked.

At that question, he leaned back and pulled his hand away.

"Did I say something wrong?" Surprised, the pitch of her voice rose.

"No. But that is a very serious question and requires a very serious answer." Finn took a deep breath. "My people are dying. Not today, not tomorrow, but within a generation. We opened the portals in an attempt to stop it."

Sadie drew her arms close and retracted a little on the couch. She looked at him as if she hoped there was a punchline to the joke she had yet to hear. But there was nothing funny about his people's situation.

"Like you're sick?" Sadie sounded empathetic.

"No, not sick, just broken. Our people are living longer than on Earth. We're stronger. Healthier," he tried to reassure her fears. "But we're also not producing female children. At first, they thought it was a...I believe Princess Eve said the word was flute, fluke?"

"A fluke," Sadie supplied. "Eve is your sister-in-law, right?"

"Yes, she married my brother."

"You were saying your scholars thought your reproduction issues was a fluke?"

"Yes, at first, our scholars thought it was a fluke, and couples were encouraged to produce large families, to have as many children as they could in hopes that females would appear again. Only, it didn't work. Now, we have even more men and no women for them to mate with. As this vast generation gets older, they want what our parents have. They want to create families and have wives. They want love.

And, as a member of the Draig royal family, it is my responsibility to help them find it."

"You can't be held responsible for biological abnormalities. You didn't cause this," Sadie defended him even though he did not need it.

"But, I am responsible. As is my brother, Kyran, and my parents, and Princes Rafe and Ivar, and their parents. Just as you, as my wife, are now responsible. They look to us to lead. For their sake, we must find them brides. Draig and Var historical documents indicate that humans are reproductively compatible. We unearthed the portal and went back to our former planet to prove this correct."

"You expect me to..." Sadie frowned. "What? How in the world, or planet, or universe, can I help an entire population of dragon-shifters find wives? It's not like the Earth government is going to listen to me when I try to tell them the idea."

"We are not contacting the Earth government."

Sadie gave a small nod. "Yeah, after my little portal trip, I didn't think so."

"I regret the way you were treated," Finn said. "Prince Ivar and I were having a disagreement, and you were not meant to see that."

"I'm sorry, but this secret can't be revealed," Sadie whispered.

"You're right. We cannot tell anyone about—"

"No, that's what Ivar said to me before he threw me here," Sadie interrupted.

"What else did he tell you?" Finn leaned forward, desperate to figure out a way to help Ivar, to know that he was safe.

"Nothing. Just that he was sorry." Sadie bit her lip and slid her leg off the couch, she stood, putting distance between them. "I don't see what you need me to do about any of this. I operate a food and travel website. I live off the advertising. I'm not a match-maker. I'm not about to go through a portal to other worlds to help you grab women purely for sex."

"We have made mistakes," Finn allowed. "A day is not much time to find a woman and convince her to come home with us. I admit we knew the plan was extreme, but we were overly optimistic when we started this project, perhaps too hopeful. We never meant to kidnap anyone against their will. We would never go against the will of the gods in such a way. Our plan was to sneak to Earth, walk around, find our mates and come home. Because of the contro-versy surrounding the idea, Kyran, Ivar, Rafe, and I were to go through and find brides. We were to prove this could work. We watched your television trans-missions and sent scouts through to gather information. We thought we knew what we were doing. We have since learned that we were making fools of ourselves. Our first night through we told everyone we were drag queens. We thought it meant royalty."

At that Sadie chuckled. The sound caused the ache inside of his chest to lessen. It gave him a small hope that she might understand the importance of what he was saying.

"And you see no other way?" she asked.

"The few alien species that have come here to make contact have not proven themselves to be proper mating material. They're either incompatible or have conflicting customs that are not harmonious with our ways, or they simply have no desire to live on this planet." Finn stood before her, wanting to close the distance between them. Every part of him was pulled in her direction, like a driving force that recognized her importance to his survival. "Many of the elders, including Lord Montague, are not happy with the portal being open. They keep reciting examples from the old days, spreading fear amongst any who would listen. They wish to close the portal permanently. They have been looking for any excuse to make that happen. With only half of the princes showing success, and then the fact that several of the dragon-shifter people have snuck away to Earth never to be heard from again, well…" He gave a help-less gesture. "It took decades to put this plan into motion. We can't stop it now."

"What about the Var?"

"The cat-shifter people are not as frightened about interacting with aliens as the dragons are, and they seem to have accepted the idea better than we have. However, the portal is on Draig land, and many of my people feel this gives us the right to control it. The Var aren't happy about that. Relations have become strained between our people. Now, with Prince Ivar stranded on Earth…"

"You're afraid this will start a war?" Sadie nodded. "I can see that. Historically speaking wars have started over less."

"No, no, not a war. That can't happen," Finn shook his head in denial. "But this will not help tensions between both sides."

"So I ask again. What do you expect me to do about any of this? Do you want me to tell your parents that it wasn't your fault? I already did that. I told them Ivar hit you and threw you in. I can say the same to Ivar's parents if you think it will help."

Finn felt a sadness wash over him. "You must promise me you will never repeat what I am about to reveal to you."

Sadie looked worried, but she nodded. "Ok."

"When shifters find their mate, it is said something happens inside of them. One look and they know as sure as anything. We had thought exposure to many women would make our task easy. Only two of the four of us found wives in such a way. The elders are calling this plan a failure and are going to close the portals. I convinced Ivar that we would go one last time and find women, any women, willing to marry us—true mate or not. What I didn't tell him is if that didn't happen, I planned on staying behind on Earth. With me there, they couldn't close them down until the portal reopened where I was stranded. It would buy time to come up with a better solution."

"That's what you were fighting about. You wanted to stay. Ivar wasn't having it. And he got trapped, left behind because I interfered." Sadie walked toward the fireplace and rested her forehead against the mantel, and stared into the flames. "So, it's my fault everything is messed up. I should have minded my own business."

"You thought you were doing the right thing. You faced a great warrior because you thought someone needed help. It was very noble of you. I am proud to call you my wife."

"But you didn't feel that thing when you saw me,

did you?" Sadie glanced up at him. She looked sad. "When it comes down to it, that's what you're too scared to admit to me, isn't it? You want me to stay here as your wife, but you don't feel connected to me as a shifter should."

"I'm sorry," Finn shook his head. "I like you. I am very attracted to you, but I worry that part of myself may be broken. I'm sure we can come to love each other. I will make you a good husband, Sadie. I will give you everything I have. I will be loyal. I will search the galaxies to fulfill your every wish. Please, stay with me. Make everyone believe that this marriage is ordained by the gods and that you're happy. Help me keep the portal open. Help me save the dragons."

9

Sadie stared at Finn, unsure of which emotion gripped her more. Was it disbelief or disappointment? Finn was offering her a marriage of convenience. The notion went against every convention of a modern woman. After all, that was what her parents had, mostly. Sure, they had loved each other, but her mom was a military wife who, as her father often explained it, "kept the home operating like a well-oiled machine," while he, "protected our nation, our values, and our way of life."

Bestowed with the same sense of responsibility, probably even more so than her dad, Finn had a lot of the same qualities she'd been raised to believe in—he talked of duty, and of preserving a way of life.

Besides the guarded front door, Finn's home was comprised of a series of doorless rooms joined by open arches. The windows were narrow, too small to fit through, but wide enough to get a view of the mountain range and treetops beyond the castle. The furniture appeared carved and sewn by hand, with an attention to detail that usually only the wealthy could afford. Weapons hung on a wall like a museum display that belonged behind velvet ropes. All the swords, axes, and knives sharpened to a gleam as if ready for battle.

Through one arch was a small kitchen. It had a stove grate over a fire pit, and an array of odd appliances she couldn't wait to figure out how to use. The refrigerator was through a hatch in the floor. The counters had been carved from stone and merely appeared an eccentric version of Earth homes. She couldn't say the same for the bathroom. The long bench that served as a toilet had been a little daunting. And the bath was an indoor natural spring that never seemed to stop bubbling.

She was living inside a fantasy movie set.

Only it was real.

Staring at these rooms for two days, watching sun after sun pass over the top dome, seeing exotic birds land on the other side of the window looking in at her as if she were an exhibit, it had been hard to deny that she was indeed on another planet and staying with royalty. She'd even found Finn's crown amongst his belongings. Not that she's set out from day one to snoop, but the days were long and drawn out with little or nothing for her to do.

"You're not speaking," Finn observed as if he had to break the long silence.

"I was thinking how big your home is," she said. "And it is only one part of this palace."

"I know it is the smaller of the royal rooms, but I did not need more space. My brother, as the future king, had need of the large suite. Where I have a bedroom, he has an office. His room is reached by stairs to separate it from the rest of his home. That way when visitors wish to meet with him, he never has to worry if the servants have tended his bed or not."

"You misunderstand. I'm not saying it's small. I'm saying it's huge. It's bigger than any apartment or extended stay hotel I've ever lived in as an adult. I'm sure it is larger than any of my childhood homes. Though, I will say I like having someone else make my bed for me. That's why extended stays are so great. Housekeeping."

"You wish for smaller? I can find you smaller,"

Finn offered. "I meant it when I said I want to make you happy."

"For me to even consider giving this a shot, there is one thing I need from you." Sadie crossed over to the large pull strings hanging down from the center dome and pulled one to close the curtain overhead. It cast the home into darkness.

"Anything." He stood. The orange light from the fireplace illuminated him in a way that was all too sexy. Watching him sleep had been torture, seeing the curve of his hip molded by silky blankets, memorizing the slope of his nose, and recalling the feel of his lips to hers. The loose shirt hid more than it revealed.

Sadie pressed her hand against the center of his chest. The steady beat of his heart beneath her fingers reminded her of how real this moment was. She wasn't scared of sex, or dragons, or alien worlds. Change did not frighten her. It was permanence that terrified her—staying in the same place, talking to the same people who would eventually learn all her secrets and annoying habits and in the end reject her because of them.

First meets are easy. Staying is hard.

Finn offered her very noble reasons to be his

wife, to remain on this planet, to become a princess who never had to worry about where the next meal or advertiser would come from. But he didn't love her. Perhaps that was all right though. Would she have believed him if he said those three words under the current circumstances?

"What do you need?" he asked.

Sadie lifted on her toes and kissed him. Her hands glided into his hair to hold him close. Being with him felt natural. The loose shirt moved seductively between them as she pushed her body against his chest.

Finn made a small noise of approval and wrapped his arms around her back. Hands cupped her ass, and he lifted her from the ground and carried her the short distance to the couch. He set her dangling feet back on the floor and then pulled away to tug his shirt over his head and toss it aside. His muscles danced erotically beneath his skin as he reached for her gown. He pulled it over her head just as enthusiastically.

Sadie reached behind her back to unlatch her bra. The warm fire felt wonderful against her naked flesh, but not as nice as when her breasts touched him for the first time. A shiver ran over her, causing her knees to weaken. She lost her footing and fell back onto the couch.

Finn took her lack of grace as an invitation and leaned over her. His hand and knee pressed into the cushion, bracing his weight so he could explore the length of her body. Fingers glided over her side, touching her skin as if memorizing her curves. He caressed down her thigh before moving upward.

A tingling sensation worked over her body, and her breath caught. Her hand ran over his chest, feeling the solid thud of his heart. Pleasure erupted everywhere he touched. His scent surrounded her. When he looked at her, his eyes shifted and changed, the gold flash in their depths mesmerizing her.

His finger hooked onto her panties, and he gently pulled them off her hip. He watched her face as if waiting for any show of hesitancy or doubt. Sadie pulled the material on the opposite hip and dragged the lacy underwear down her legs to help him undress her.

He leaned back, pulling them off her feet. Fire-light added both eroticism and romance to the moment. It softened his features while highlighting the effects of his arousal. Finn lifted her foot and kissed the arch before trailing his lips along her leg. Each worshipping caress was carefully placed.

Her eyes roamed his body, looking for anything abnormal. Aside from his flashing eyes, he looked very human—a sexy, smoldering hot human.

"Come here. There's time for play later. Right now, I want you." She reached for his neck, urging him to crawl along her body. He kissed her hip before moving up.

"Whatever my lady wishes," he said before rubbing his lips against hers. "Your wish is my command."

She wiggled until his legs were resting between hers. His thick arousal bumped her thigh as he maneuvered his hips forward. There was a slight moment of fear overshadowed by anticipation as the tip of his cock slid along her wet opening. Desire had never felt like this, like lava in her veins, like stars bursting around her vision, like... like...

"Finn," she whispered. She pressed her hips up, desperate to be filled.

His primal growl answered her weak cry as he slid deep. The fear left her. This was what she wanted, this feeling, this moment, the aching climax just beyond her reach. Sadie clawed at his ass, keeping him deep when he would withdraw. He circled his hips.

She wanted to make it last, but her body had

other plans. The days spent staring at his sleeping form had taken their toll. She needed this. She needed him.

"Finn," she gasped, barely able to form the word. The muscles inside her clamped over him. He thrust deeper. She orgasmed hard, the mindless drive too much to resist. Within seconds, Finn was coming with her. He looked almost surprised by the suddenness of it, but there was no stopping fate.

Weakened in the aftermath of pleasure, she dropped her legs to the side and endeavored to catch her breath. "Wow, Finn, I mean, wow."

He leaned back, with only a smile on his features. His lips parted to answer, but a knock sounded on the door. She braced herself at the interruption. The door began to open, and someone spoke in the Draig language.

Finn yelled something in response. He shot up from the couch and grabbed her dress. He tossed it over her body. "The food." He rushed to the door naked.

Stunned, Sadie pulled the gown over her chest and watched as a naked Finn gathered the tray. She gave a small laugh when he turned. "That was close."

The door pushed open behind him. Her laughter

died to see the queen behind her son. The woman slammed the door and began to speak, only to stutter to stop when she witnessed Finn's ass. She made a strange noise and turned. Sadie didn't need to speak the language to know when someone was being scolded.

"Would someone mind translating for me?" Sadie asked.

Finn gave her a half smile. "She told me to dress myself. That this is no way to answer a door."

"Good, you're both here," the queen said, not turning around as she still faced the door. "Maybe one of you could tell me what it is you're thinking, though I think it's obvious that neither one of you have given much thought as to what this arrangement looks like. People are saying this marriage is cursed because—"

"What people?" Finn asked.

Sadie hastily dressed. The woman's appearance worked better than an ice shower.

"Everyone—the servants, the elders, the guards," the queen answered. "They all saw what happened. I mean, honestly? What possessed you to get married like that? In that... that... rag."

"No law says the marriage tent needs to be of the

finest quality," Finn defended. He set down the tray and grabbed his pants. As he slid his legs in, he continued, "It just needs to be a tent, a symbol of shared household." He tied a drawstring at his waist. "You can turn around now."

The queen peeked over her shoulder before moving to face her son fully. She glanced over him and gave a small nod. Finn returned the gesture. The queen pointed her attention to Sadie who stood by the couch. Sadie smoothed down her hair, conscious about how she must have looked in such an awkward moment.

"And you. What kind of woman would allow a man to treat her like that? A dirty blanket pinned to the side of the mountain?" The queen arched a brow. She looked frightful.

Sadie opened her mouth, but words failed her. She took a deep breath as anger built inside at the thought of this woman presumed she had the right to scold her like some naughty kid. Why was she scared of her? Was it because she was "queen." The hard looks and tone were nothing compared to when her father disciplined Sadie as a child.

"Well?" the queen demanded. "Don't you have anything to say for yourself?"

"What kind of woman am I? I'll tell you what

kind." Sadie put her hands on her hips to hide their shaking. Nerves bunched her stomach and heated her cheeks, but she answered anyway. "I'm the kind that doesn't put on airs. The kind who doesn't care about the finery of a ceremony. Maybe you should reexamine what's lacking in your own life, and figure out why it's so important to you to be surrounded by material objects. You might have married for money and pretty things, but I didn't. I prefer people to jewels, but then, that may be just me. You want to judge me? Go ahead. But do it somewhere else because we were in the middle of something more important than this conversation."

The queen stared at her for a long moment.

Shit.

Maybe Sadie had pushed it too far. An apology was on the tip of her tongue, but she resisted the urge.

"Finally," the queen answered, the word clipped. "One of you boys found an Earth woman with some dragon fire in her. When you're shown any doubt, answer with that much conviction, but fewer insults. That passion for your choice will quiet the wagging tongues." And then she turned her attention to her son.

Finn grinned.

"Come find me after you're done here. We have important matters to discuss." The queen touched her son's cheek. "I'm glad you are well. Never act that foolish again."

Finn nodded and opened the door for his mother. He shut it decisively behind her.

"What was that speech about?" Finn asked. "You had nothing to do with the tent choice. You could have told her that I insulted your honor by offering you such a poor ceremony."

"She didn't know that, and I'm sorry, but she pissed me off. Money isn't everything. I'm not rich, and I've never been ashamed of it. I work hard. I pay my bills. I—"

"You are beautiful," Finn put forth as if he couldn't contain himself. "And you quieted my mother. I have never seen anyone win her affection so quickly."

"*That* was affection?" Sadie gave a small laugh of disbelief.

"She said you had dragon spirit. That's very high praise." Finn pulled the draw string at his waist. "Now, don't mention her again, at least not now. I believe we were in the middle of something very important."

His eyes flashed with gold and Sadie cried out in surprise when he leaped for her. He gave another playful lunge and a growl. She took off running toward his bed and didn't look back.

10

SADIE'S ARM twitched as she tried shaking off the annoying tapping on her forearm. After a night filled with intense, mind-altering pleasure, every muscle in her body was relaxed, and the last thing she wanted was to wake from the pleasant fog of her dreams. But the tapping became insistent.

Sadie grumbled as she opened her eyes. She jolted in surprise, stiffening, as a woman's face hovered over hers. Long, straight, dark brown hair had streaks of blue through it. Her hazel green eyes sparkled.

"Shh," the woman mouthed. Her friendly smile looked more playful than threatening. She held up a fistful of clothing. "Put this on, and..." The unknown woman tilted her head toward the front door.

Sadie arched a brow. She turned to look at where Finn lay sleeping.

"Hello, Eve," Finn said, not opening his eyes.

"Hey. I'm kidnapping your wife," Eve answered. She dropped the clothes on the bed and stood. "Queen mother lifted the guards from your door. Otherwise, I would have done it sooner."

Finn opened one eye. He appeared wide awake as he focused on her. "Do you wish to be kidnapped?"

Sadie gestured helplessly. "I—"

"Sure she does, Finn," Eve answered for her. "You're not going to make her stay cooped up in this place for another day, are you?"

"I do not make her do anything," Finn answered.

"Smart man." Eve chuckled. "Rise and shine, princess. If we don't sneak out now, we'll be roped into royal duties."

Eve moved toward the kitchen and disappeared through the arched doorway.

"Should we be worried that she was watching us sleep?" Sadie asked.

"Eve means no harm. She's probably excited to have another female in the palace. She's been begging me to marry for a long while now." Finn smiled as he reached for her shoulder to give her a light caress. "She is right, though. The queen will have you fitted for dresses and listening to etiquette coaches all morning. Then there are the historians, and meeting the elders, and—"

"I'm coming, Eve." Sadie shook a leg as she tried to untangle her feet from the covers.

The clothes Eve brought her were surprisingly Earth trendy. The soft leggings had a bright dragon pattern on them, and the dress was more of an oversized black t-shirt. The woman even supplied clean underwear. When she glanced back at the bed, Finn was watching her dress with a goofy smile on his face. "What?"

"The queen will hate that you're dressed like Eve," Finn answered, not appearing at all worried.

"Ready?" Eve called, coming out of the kitchen holding a goblet. She took a drink before setting it down on the mantel.

"Almost," Eve glanced around for her bra.

Eve reached toward the couch and then held up the lacy undergarment. "Looking for this?"

"Yes, thank you." Sadie grabbed the bra and threaded her arms into the t-shirt to put it on under her clothes. Considering all the strange things she'd been forced to accept, this interchange with Princess Eve was one of the least odd.

Eve politely turned her attention away. Finn did not. He sat on the bed, staring at her as if fascinated by her strange ritual.

"This open bedroom, living room, house plan will take some getting used to," Sadie stated. "I'm not sure I like the bed being out on display like it is."

"I tried to tell him that was weird for a palace," Eve offered. "But apparently, several of the suites are set up like this."

"Kind of loft New York apartment, only less industrial," Sadie observed.

"Mm, I miss New York." Eve gave a wistful sigh. "They have this little rundown food truck with the best hamburgers known to man."

"*Hackfleisch Rectangular Garden?*"

"Yes! You know it?"

"I did a story about their burgers a couple of years ago," Sadie said. "So good."

"Right? I dream about that burger." Eve held her hand over her chest and gave another sigh. "I miss fast food so much—going to get fries and shakes at three in the morning after a gig."

"I bring you burgers," Finn said from the bed, as if not to be left out of the conversation.

"You don't understand the complexity of burger shopping," Eve dismissed. She hooked her arm through Sadie's. "My shoes might be a size too big for you, but I brought you some sandals." She motioned to the floor by the door.

Sadie slipped her feet in. The fit wasn't too off. "I'm taking that to mean they don't do hamburgers here?"

"No. They're all healthy—fresh fruit this, blue bread that." Eve opened the door. "I miss bacon. And diner coffee. And cheese fries. Oh, what I wouldn't do for a plate of cheese fries with bacon."

"I could go for a pizza," Sadie said. It was what was supposed to be on her menu schedule for today—a pie from a Russian-ran pizzeria, and then later one from a local music venue in downtown Oxford.

"Now you're talking!" Eve exclaimed. "Pizza for breakfast, you are my kind of girl."

"You're a princess?" Sadie asked, eyeing the blue hair. "I have to admit that you don't look like I pictured a princess would look."

Eve touched the locks. "I hid my tiara."

"Hey, don't keep her too long," Finn called. "I wish to—"

"Oh, that reminds me, I almost forgot to tell you. Your brother needs you to meet him in an hour at the council chamber. Something about the rumors that you and Ivar took an unsanctioned trip and tried to abduct a village of..." Eve attempted to speak the local language, before finishing "which I think translates into low-class, diseased women."

"I'm not diseased!" Sadie gasped.

Finn held the blanket around his waist and made his way from the bed toward the front door. He gripped the covers with one hand and placed the other on Sadie's arm. "I promise I will see that this affront to your honor is stopped at once. There will be no more rumors about my bride."

"Uh, thanks," Sadie said, unsure about the fierceness of his response.

"Ok, we need to get going before the queen finds us. We'll be outside in the village, Finn, don't worry."

"Don't take it personally," Eve said as she led her out of the door. "They thought I was a mutant because I color my hair blue. My husband told me they were worried our children would end up with blue hair."

"Oh, how many do you have?"

"None. I'm not ready for motherhood." Eve pulled the door shut and motioned that they should head down a long stone hallway. "Maybe someday. But I'm sure that's part of the problem. The people are worried about compatibility and having babies with mates that these rumors about you being diseased are manifestations of their fears. Jenna, who married the cat-shifter prince, Rafe, has not had children either. So they think all human women are broken."

"I'm not ready for children," Sadie said. "Nothing about my life says kids. I travel. I live out of hotel rooms."

Eve gave a glance back at Finn's room. "So, you're not sure you're staying?"

"I don't know. It's a lot to take in," Sadie answered.

"I get that. The way I look at it, Qurilixen is like a foreign country. People on Earth evolved differently depending on their environments, right? Dark or light skin, light or dark eyes, various biological features and adaptations, different languages and customs. The shape-shifter people evolved into human dragons and cats. Their ancestral tribe struck out exploring, discovered this new territory through a portal, and there you have it. A medieval-like society with dragon-shifters and cat-shifters running around."

Sadie thought about Eve's simple yet perfect explanation for the way things were on Qurilixen. "That actually makes me feel a little better." She glanced around the halls. "This palace looks like a cross between a medieval castle and the Roman Empire. The sculptures and paintings I've seen in the palace look like they belong in the museum. I feel like if I touch something alarms will go off. Just don't tell me they have gladiator fights."

"Not that I've seen. It's all very civilized, or at least it has been." Eve led the way, absently touching items as she walked by them. Her fingers glanced over a woven tapestry, making it flutter against the wall. The embroidered scene depicted flying dragons fighting tiny human men.

"You say that like things are about to change." Sadie lifted her finger to touch a sewn dragon. It felt wrong making physical contact with something so magnificent. She withdrew her hand. "Is that what they look like fully shifted?"

"None that I've seen. The men look more like dragon men than full blooded medieval dragons. The queen doesn't shift in front of me, except to do that eye flashing thing when she's irritated. My husband told me that Queen Galina is one of the last female dragons born and her fiery temper runs hotter than any dragon-shifter man if you get her riled up." Eve grinned. "You like fine art? Come check this out." She quickly turned a corner and pointed up into a small alcove.

Sadie looked up at the painting and laughed. Stretched black velvet had been painted to depict a semi-truck with a floating head behind it. Plastic gemstones decorated the cheap gold-colored frame. "Is that a velvet trucker Elvis?"

"I found it for sale in New Orleans and had to have it." Eve laughed harder. "I hung it here as a joke and didn't say anything. I think everyone's too afraid of offending me to take it down. Makes me laugh every time."

"That's almost too hideous to hate," Sadie said.

Eve laughed harder. "I like you. I hope you consider staying. This family could use more human women in it."

"What about your Earth family? Do they know where you are?"

"The only family I need is here," Eve said. Sadie guessed by the woman's expression that there was more to that story, but didn't pry. "Is that why you want to go back? Family?"

"My mother. We don't see each other a lot, but we talk on the phone about once a month. I'm not the stay in one place type. I like moving around."

"Aw, well, no worries. You don't have to decide right now." She paused as the sound of footsteps approached and pulled Sadie into the Elvis alcove to hide and pressed her finger to her lips. She waited until the sound moved away before glancing around the corner to check if the coast was clear. "They're gone. Come on." She continued down the hall. "Trust me when I tell you not to go around saying your doubts too loudly while you're here. It will cause a lot of problems. They're into the whole will of the gods, fated mate thing."

"And I take it you're not convinced?"

"Oh, no, I am," Eve corrected. "I am right where I was meant to be—married to Kyran. When you know, you know. And when dragons know, they genuinely know. I might miss singing with my band on stage and eating hamburgers whenever I want, but that would be nothing compared to the heartache of losing my husband."

Sadie hid the pain that washed over her. She could see how much the woman adored her husband when she talked about him. Sadly, Finn had already warned Sadie that she wasn't his fated mate, or true love, or whatever one wanted to call it. The attraction between them was fierce and powerful. Even now it hummed through her body, causing her toes to curl and her breathing to deepen in anticipation. But lust was not love, and Finn wouldn't fall in love with her.

"I didn't invite you out this morning to put pressure on you," Eve said. "It wasn't even my intention to get into all of this, but now that we have I have to say something."

"About?"

"The portal." Eve stopped walking. She touched the leg of a statue and ran her finger along the stone calf. "It's important that we do all we can to keep it open. Selfishly, it's my only way to visit Earth, or else I might get homesick. Not so selfishly, it's the only hope the shifters have for survival. I know it must sound horrible—their going to Earth like cavemen to capture brides and drag them back here. But it's not like that. When a dragon man knows, he knows. It's nature, and biology, and chemicals, and fate, and I can't explain it very well, but it is real. I have yet to hear about an unhappy marriage. I wish there were a way to visibly show what I'm saying so I can prove how real it is. Like a ray of light joining two people. Or twinkling stardust raining over a couple's head whenever they are near each other like fairy powder."

They neared a barred gate with metal spear tips linking the bottom. It was lifted a few feet off the ground. Beyond the gate were two closed wooden doors.

Eve hummed thoughtfully to herself. "I've never seen these doors shut before."

As they approached, two guards stepped out of the shadows. Eve pointed to a row of knobs on the wall. "See these?"

Sadie nodded.

"Show Princess Sadie the barrier," Eve commanded.

The guards looked at each other and didn't readily move.

"Ah, come on. I know you all heard about my run-in with the guard shield." Eve laughed, before turning to Sadie. "It's like an invisible electric fence. I walked right into it. Zapped the hell out of me, threw me to the floor, knocked me unconscious, and blistered the tip of my nose, so I looked like one of Santa's reindeer."

One of the guard's mouth twitched as if he tried to hold back his amusement.

"Oh, go ahead and laugh," Eve told the man. "It was funny."

Finally, one of the guards leaned over, plucked a pebble from the ground and tossed it toward Eve. The stone hit an electrical wall and entered the force field. Zapping noises and small bolts of energy flashed lighting up the area. Sadie gasped as she jumped back.

"Just be careful when trying to leave the palace," Eve instructed. She reached to push at a stone in the wall. The transparent shield tinted with blue. Eve stepped into the blue light, showing Sadie it was now safe to cross, before dipping under the half-raised gate and going forward. "Thanks, fellas."

"We are not supposed to let anyone leave," a guard said, not stepping aside.

"Under whose order?" Eve demanded.

"Lord Montague," the man answered.

All pleasantness faded from Eve's expression. "I'm sure he didn't mean to dictate the freedoms of a princess of the House of Draig."

They again shared a look, but still didn't move.

"Step aside by royal order. I will not ask again," Eve insisted.

The men spoke softly to each other in the Draig language before one opened the front door. Eve took Sadie by the arm and led her past the guards and out into the sunlight.

"That Lord Montague sounds like a real character," Sadie said, watching the door to the palace shut behind them. The green daylight turned Eve's blue hair into an even deeper shade. It reflected off her face and neck, giving an almost cinematic quality to her skin tone.

"He's an asshole," Eve stated, direct and to the point. "I'm convinced he's behind all the rumors being spread around about Earth and the portal stops. He has been lobbying to get them shut down since before I came here. So what if a few dragon men decided they wanted to move away from home? It's their lives. They're the ones making the decisions and taking the risks. They should be able to leave if they choose."

The palace castle stood over the valley. Eve gestured that Sadie should follow her down to a nearby village. They walked along the edge of a forest that hugged around the small cottages and patches of farmland. Specs of yellow dotted the bushes. Cobblestone paths joined houses on the hill-side. "It's like stepping back in time, isn't it? Only cleaner than I'd imagine the Middle Ages to be. Or onto a movie set. Medieval village, take one." Eve pushed her hands forward and then stretched her arms wide to encompass the scene like a director. "Cue the dragon men leaving their homes to work the fields, toiling under the three suns to grow the grain to make blue bread, who must fight against the tyranny of—"

"The crazy Lord Montague," Sadie supplied in a dramatic voice.

Eve laughed, hard. She nodded her head. "Can you believe that man's nerve? Trying to forbid us from leaving the palace. I'm sorry, I love my prince husband, but I'm my own person, and I come and go as I please. I'd like to think that's what he loves about me."

Sadie's smile fell, as she again thought of what Finn said. One fact played over and over in her brain —she was not his true love. That didn't mean she wasn't already falling for him. The pull she felt toward Finn was unlike any attraction she'd ever known. Even now the feel of his lips were ghosted imprints on her skin, branding her as his.

"Listen to me joking around when you must have a lot of questions. I know I did. I had so many I didn't know where to even begin. First, don't let the shifter part frighten you. It's not like the wolf man. They don't go all crazy on the full moon. They don't have full moons here. They can control the change. They shift when they want to, or automatically as a form of bodily protection—like if they were to fall off a cliff or be attacked by a knife."

Sadie let the woman talk, unsure if Eve was trying to convince her to stay, trying to put her at ease, or simply trying to fill the silence. Perhaps Eve had been without Earth company for so long that the words flowed in an unstoppable gush of excitement.

"My husband tried to tell me that a female dragon can fly, but I've never seen it." Eve laughed. "Come to think of it, my husband said he's never seen it either. I doubt it's true, which is a pity. That would be awesome to see. Also, a pity is the fact that shifting is not contagious. I so wanted to be a dragon and fly, but apparently once a human always a human."

Sadie took a deep breath. The smell of cotton candy and vanilla cookies filled her nose. It carried on the breeze as if coming from the grasses or trees. Mountains surrounded the palace and village, their tall spiked peaks pointing toward the sky. It was like an underground giant had reached up from the earth to cradle the city in his hand.

This moment felt important, like standing on the edge of a cliff deciding whether or not to jump. Strange sounds came from within the trees. The skinny trunks were covered with bubble-textured bark.

"Birds," Eve explained when she saw Sadie turn toward the sound. "Everything is just close enough to Earth to be recognizable, and just alien enough to be strange." She paused and waved as she neared a group of farmers. They wore the tunic shirts and pants in the same style she'd seen on those in the palace. "Murdock, come, meet Princess Sadie!"

"I'm not a princess," Sadie denied, trying to keep her voice low.

"If you're not taken, you're on the market," Eve said. "Do you want to be on the market? Or is it safe to assume you're cool hanging out as Finn's woman for now?"

"Uh, I'm, ah, cool hanging as Finn's friend," Sadie answered. Eve had a unique way of talking to get her point across.

"Well you come," Murdock stated as he approached.

"Welcome," Eve whispered in translation.

"Thank you," Sadie said. "Nice to meet you. I'm Sadie."

"I am Muireadhach," the farmer said.

"Don't even try to say it. Call him Murdock," Eve suggested.

"Yes, Princess Eve says I am a Murdock," Muireadhach allowed. "And may I say, Princess Sadie, you are a quite bitchin' babe."

Sadie's mouth opened, but she wasn't sure how to answer.

"Your language is coming along nicely," Eve praised the man.

"Thank you," Muireadhach grinned. "Princess Eve has been teaching me to blend for when I am allowed to cross over the portal."

"Rock-n-roll." Eve threw a couple of fingers into the air.

"Rock-n-roll," the man repeated the gesture as if it was a suitable way to say goodbye.

Sadie arched a brow.

"What?" Eve shrugged. "He wanted to learn to be cool."

"And that other stoic guy behind him staring at us like he couldn't be bothered?" Sadie asked.

"No English. That's Beringer. He married one of the last dragon-shifter females so feels no need to speak our words. You'll find a lot of the married men are like that. They have their mates, so they're not looking to talk to other females." Eve waved at the man. He gestured politely in kind before waving Murdock back toward the fields.

Eve continued her tour of the village, introducing Sadie as a princess to everyone they came across. The people appeared to have a real affection for her, all but a few of the married men who kept back. None of the single men tried to flirt with them, which Sadie found strange for a planet full of guys who didn't have women around. Then again, she kept thinking about Finn back in his bed and didn't try flirting with any of them.

Between greetings, Eve explained how the planet was divided in half. The Var cat-shifters lived to the south of the dragons. Each shifter population stayed on their side of the planet—not because they fought, but because they had different ways of doing things. Eve had never heard of a dragon-shifter and cat-shifter having a baby, but supposed they would make a bizarre creature.

"Fluffy dragon or hairless cat," Eve had supposed with another of her playful laughs.

If that weren't terrifying enough, aliens from outer space would sometimes visit. In the west, they were breaking ground on some ore mines to make an intergalactic trade. It was going to be a long time before operations were set up—perhaps even generations.

By the time they made their way back toward the palace, Sadie felt she had a reasonable sense of the planet and the people. Eve had done her best to convince her she needed to stay and help keep the portals open. None of that mattered.

There was one thing Eve didn't realize her tour

had revealed. The dragon couples loved each other very much. The adoration when Beringer looked at his wife, when any of them looked at their wives, was potent and strong. They didn't need a ray of light or sprinklings of fairy dust. The love was there for all to see. How could Sadie agree to stay married to Finn and keep him from finding such pure happiness for himself with his true mate? And an even harder question—how could she live with him knowing she could never be who he was destined for?

Sadie pondered these things, mulling them over in her mind, and the more she thought about them, the more her feelings for Finn deepened.

11

FINN STARED down the long palace hall, wanting nothing more than to go to the village and find Sadie. He worried about her, about what Eve was telling her about him, about her being in the village around unmated men. What if she found her true mate? What if she left him? The pain he felt at that idea was real.

Finn knew he had a reputation for not taking things seriously because he often tried to lighten the mood with jokes and laughter. No more. He was married now. He needed to realize his potential. For himself. For his people. For Sadie. She deserved a husband she could be proud of.

With his goal in mind, he turned his attention to the council chamber door and waited.

"You're early," his brother Kyran acknowledged, not bothering to hide the surprise in his blue gaze. His black hair was pulled back from his face. "I thought I would have to drag you to this meeting."

"Of course I came," Finn answered. "It's my duty to be here."

Kyran gave him a perplexed look before carefully answering, "Care to tell me what happened before we go in there? Are there any truths to the rumors?"

"My wife is not diseased," Finn stated. He balled his fists in warning, ready to take on anyone who tried to claim such a thing.

"I know that." Kyran lifted is hands as if to tell his brother to take it easy. His voice lowered to a hush. "That much goes without saying. What I meant is there anything to the rumors about Ivar?"

"What are people saying?"

"Many things." Kyran didn't try to lighten the gossipmongers' words, as he said, "That you lured Ivar through the portal and then killed him on the other side. You both took an unsanctioned trip and tried to abduct a village of graveyard bound woman in a desperate move to distract the elders. That the two of you went through, met with trouble, and you abandoned him like a coward. That you defied the will of the gods. That you stumbled out into the prairie broken and bloody, and chased a screaming human woman. That Ivar did not come back at all. You did it because of a woman. You did it because you are jealous of Ivar. You did it because—"

"Enough," Finn stopped him. "How are such things being said so quickly? There were only a handful of men who saw me come back from the trip. Only a few of them could know about Sadie running and screaming when she first arrived. Ivar had just thrown her through the portal without warning. Can we blame her for being a little shaken?"

"Then one of the guards on duty that night is the one spreading the rumors. Who all were there?"

"Gudmund, Cleve, Albin, Cedar, Gale, Jaron..." Finn motioned weakly. "Then whoever rode out with our parents and Lord Montague, but all of them came later after the marriage tent. Cedar and Gale don't speak the Earth language, so they probably heard nothing worth repeating. Plus they did not come too close to Sadie. They did search the tunnels for Ivar before realizing he didn't make it back from the other side."

"I trained with them. And with Albin. They're loyal, and not ones for gossip," Kyran said. "I doubt Jaron would spread rumors. He's in line to be one of the first through the portal to find a mate if and when travel opens. He has spoken out many times at the public meetings to keep the portal open."

"Cleve is young and eager to prove himself worthy of the post," Finn dismissed. "I think this was the first unmated woman the lad had ever seen. I don't perceive him as talking out of turn to anyone who would listen."

"Do you think... Gudmund?" Kyran frowned. "I have not had many interactions with Gudmund. I always had the impression he keeps his opinions close."

Finn's memories of his return were still a little jumbled after hitting his head. "Gudmund tried to convince me to hide Sadie in the Mining Camp. He seemed confident someone would take her as a wife. He appeared very worried that the Var King and Queen would be upset about Ivar."

"Naturally, that's a safe assumption," Kyran put forth. "But why would Gudmund suggest that you give away your mate? To do so would be to go against the will of the gods. We have spent weeks at the temple begging the gods to send them to us. How could he suggest you...?" Kyran paused, evidently reading something in Finn's expression. "Tell me, brother."

"I care for Sadie," Finn said, not wanting to admit

the truth. He'd told himself that no one would ever know.

"As you should," Kyran agreed. "I care for her as well, as she is part of you. She is family."

"I care for her greatly, but I do not think she is my mate. I did not have the explosion inside of me that others speak of when it happens. I don't hear her in my thoughts. I—"

"Then by all the dragons, Finn, why would you take her to your marriage tent?" Kyran exclaimed a little too loudly. He glanced around, before saying in a quieter tone, "What were you thinking? We're dragons, not Var. We do not take half mates. You bound yourself to her. You cannot have another."

Finn didn't want two wives. He wanted to know the connection of a true mate—feeling what they felt as if it were his own emotions, hearing her voice inside his head. "I did it for our people. The elders want to close the portal. Someone had to do something to stop them. Ivar agreed with me. We went to find wives. We hoped it would be mates, but any wives would have to do. This isn't about my happiness. It's about the future of the dragons."

"There's more. I see it in your eyes." Kyran narrowed is gaze.

"I did not tell Ivar this when we left, but I was

planning on not coming back. I was going to stay behind and force the elders to leave the portal open for another year."

"That is why your bag had so much Earth cash in it," Kyran concluded. "People were saying you'd gone to purchase women with the currency. Gods' bones, Finn, you are a fool. This is not some boyhood game."

"You call me a fool because I want to save our people? Tell me what should I have done? Stand aside and let our people die out?" Finn ran his fingers through his hair in frustration. He felt the scab from where he'd hit his head on the cave floor. "I tried to speak up. The king and queen would not hear me. The elders have their own agenda."

"Lord Montague wants what is best for the people," Kyran defended. "Those ideas may not line up with what we think is right. But he would not hurt the dragons."

"I did what I had to do. I feel no need to defend my actions to you, brother." Finn reached for the council chamber door. "I'm going in."

"Wait." Kyran placed a hand on Finn's arm to stop him. "I was not implying that you don't care about our people. I'm sorry I called you a fool. I'm just surprised that you would go to such an extreme. We must have faith that the gods have a plan, Finn."

"Maybe what happened is their plan. I wanted to be the one to stay behind, but they left Ivar there instead."

"I doubt the Var king and queen will see Ivar being trapped on Earth as anything but betrayal." Kyran sighed. "I know that it was not your intention, but if we do not handle this correctly, it could very well start a war between the shifters."

Finn felt the words like a kick in the gut, but how could he counter them? "I will do anything I can to make this right."

"We should speak to Gudmund," Kyran said. "See if any of the rumors emanated from him. Maybe he detected Sadie was not meant for you and was reacting. If he offered to take her to the Mining Camp maybe he had other ideas in mind. Did there seem to be anything between Gudmund and your wife?"

Finn frowned, wanting to answer that question with his fists. Nothing was happening between Gudmund and his wife. He was sure of it. Or was he? A memory flashed through his mind. Cleve had looked at Sadie the same way Finn had looked at her, full of curiosity and hope. Gudmund had an altogether different look when he looked at Sadie. The difference in Gudmund's expression could've been from the realization that this woman was not meant for the prince, and he therefore sought to separate her from Finn by any means necessary. He could not blame the man. If someone had his true mate, Finn would have done anything to steal her away.

A whirlwind of emotions filled Finn. He was angry and jealous and sad and worried all at the same time. Sadie was his wife. He did not want to lose her. The idea of her with Gudmund was almost more than he could bear. Finn wanted to punch a wall. He wanted to run through the forest in shifted form to let out some of his tension. Instead, he took a deep breath and again reached for the council chamber's door. He heard voices coming from inside.

"This is a most serious offense we are dealt. There are rumblings of foul play already starting within the Var—" At their entrance, Lord Montague stopped talking. He stood before the seated elders, arms still wide from his gesturing as he gave his political discourse. The man's pompous expression was no different than usual, but it annoyed Finn especially on this occasion. "My princes, welcome."

Montague waved his hand as he invited them into the council chamber. Yet another condescending act from the man.

"I see you started without us, even though we're early." Kyran's tone mocked the elder statesman.

"We were simply discussing an important matter that affects all of us," Montague responded.

"By all means, do continue my lord, if it cannot wait for the king and queen to join us," Kyran ordered. The censure in his voice was not lost on the gathering. He took his customary seat and folded his arms over his chest. As the oldest brother, he was the highest-ranking royal in the room.

Montague's eyes locked with Kyran's briefly in a battle of the wills before he turned back with a wide smile. "As I was saying, my friends, it affects us all when our cat-shifting neighbors are displeased. We have all come to depend on the harmony that has existed on this planet since coming here through the portal. Yes, I will not deny that there have been times of strife between our two peoples, but we have always overcome adversities by being open and honest and forthright in our dealings with the Var."

Finn grunted rudely in irritation, stopping the man from continuing. He knew that he should keep quiet for the moment but couldn't help himself as he said, "I do not think you should speak prematurely on things you do not know about. Perhaps, it would be best for you to get the facts straight, before resorting to rumors and gossip."

Kyran's eyes narrowed, and Finn knew his brother wished him to stop talking. He was openly challenging the word of the head elder, and he did so in front of council members while inside the hall. The insult was not lost an anyone, least of all Montague.

"Prince Finn, is it or is it not true that you traveled with Prince Ivar through a portal to Earth without the permission or the foreknowledge of the elders and your parents?"

Finn had no choice but to answer the direct question. He scowled at the man. "It is."

"Is it or is it not true that you invited Prince Ivar here, a foreign royal, to Draig land without the permission or the foreknowledge of the elders and your parents? And that he came without the permission or foreknowledge of the Var king and queen, a *mischievous* secret you initiated?"

Finn clenched his jaw.

"Well?"

"It is," Finn ground out from between his teeth. Montague was purposefully framing the facts in such a way that made them sound worse than they were. "But I was not aware that the royal families needed to seek the permission of the elders when no such law or forbiddance was in place. To do so would have merely been a courtesy, my lord, and by no means required."

"Finn," Kyran whispered, trying to stop him from prodding Montague's temper.

"Is it or is it not true that you returned from Earth without the Var prince?" Montague's voice rose giving away his anger toward the prince's impertinence.

"It is," Finn said.

Montague rushed on before the prince could elaborate. His voice rose to thunder over the room. "You returned bloody, undoubtedly fresh from a fight, and without Prince Ivar. The cat-shifter prince clearly had come to some harm—"

"That is not—" Finn yelled, standing from his chair. He hit his fist in the air.

"And you bring a woman—" Montague continued.

"My wife—" Finn broke in.

"A woman who has been hidden from this council's queries since her arrival, an arrival marred by her terrified screams at having witnessed what you did to the Var prince—"

"That's not—"

"A woman who allowed herself to be married under a dirty rag, and you would have us believe she is a lady worthy of ruling our great land? A woman you were only able to keep quiet by offering to make her your princess!" Montague finished with his hand held high above his head. He glared at Finn, daring him to deny it. The councilmen grumbled amongst themselves, but Finn was beyond hearing their words. By claiming Sadie was of such low character, she could be bought with a title was beyond insulting. The dragon inside him would not have it.

"When did this turn into a tribunal?" Kyran demanded.

Years of pent up anger at Montague's passive aggressive behavior of undermining the king and queen, exploded in a wild, ugly fury. Finn growled as he surged forward. His talons were drawn well before he reached the elder.

Montague still had a grin on his smug features. Finn couldn't think. Nor, could the prince reason beyond the primal need to tear out the man's offensive tongue.

How dare he say such things about his wife?

Chaos erupted around him, but Finn didn't care. Voices shouted at him to stop. Others yelled at Montague to fight back. Finn's talons met with flesh, tearing the elder's clothing as he slashed him across the arm. Montague struck violently at Finn's skull as if to aggravate his previous injury. He didn't care, even as the blows sent shockwaves of pain throughout his head. Another blow hit him just right, confusing him. Finn stumbled, dizzy, as he fought to remain conscious.

Finn's anger had no limits, and he used it for fuel as he again lunged at Montague. The more composed Montague artfully stepped to the side, sending Finn flying into a pillar.

"Brute strength is exactly that. And nothing else," Montague laughed as his cohorts naturally began to assemble around him. Since their first run in at the lake, when Finn was just a boy, Montague had made it one of his missions in life to embarrass the royal family using Finn.

Dust from the smashed pillar filled the air. Finn's shoulder ached terribly, and a small voice in the back of his mind begged him to stop. But seeing Montague smiling back at him, only made him try again. The man had insulted Sadie, and he could not let that stand. The single-minded purpose was all his dazed mind could grasp.

He knocked into the elder, sending him to the ground. Blurs flashed across his vision, and Finn felt people pulling him back, and away from Montague.

"Finn, what happened here?" King Severin demanded.

Almost instantly, Finn realized what he'd done. He'd attacked an elder in the council hall. Every implication Montague had ever made against him—about Finn being rash and impertinent, of being ill-behaved and ill-fit to rule—was proven at that moment to be true. Seeing the slight lift to Montague's mouth, Finn knew the elder had baited him into a reaction, while also imparting his political rhetoric. Once again, Montague had pushed the right button at the precise moment for Finn to flounder in front of the entire world.

Finn had sworn he could take the old man. The problem was he had not fully learned his lesson when it came to controlling his emotions and Montague relied upon that, using the prince's weakness to his advantage.

Finn's father and brother held him by the arms, as if afraid he would once more attack if released. His right arm ached from the pillar, and he tried to pull it free. Kyran did not let go.

Queen Galina stood back from the fray. She appeared regal in her stiff pose. If her chest didn't lift with breath, she could have passed as a statue. Her obvious disappointment of him was demoralizing and energy sapping.

The intricate silver embroidery edged her gown in a Qurilixian pattern. The emblem of the dragon had been sewn onto the bodice. A gold band wrapped her head. She only wore the crown for ceremonies. Though not necessarily out of place, the formal attire demonstrated just how serious his mother thought the current meeting was.

Finn glanced at his father. King Severin wore his matching long tunic with the same silver-embroidered edges and a larger dragon patch on the center of his chest. The council members were not so finely dressed, but they had noticeably come expecting an important meeting. Now they all stood in disparate pods in various locations around the room, isolating themselves from each other, protecting their beliefs and titles from tarnish and blame for what had happened.

An excitable few had jumped forward in support of Montague. While others remained near their seats, watching the scene unfold before them with bated breath and an avid curiosity as to the outcome. It was undeniable that there were some who watched hopeful for the demise of the reigning royals.

"Don't coddle me," Montague scolded his associates, shaking them off when they would help him stand.

On realizing that he'd embarrassed the prince in front of the king and queen, the elder quickly changed his tactics—acting as if he were the victim and not the cool mastermind of Finn's demise.

"It will take more than a boy to cause me harm," Montague announced, even though the blood dripping down the prince's arm indicated differently. "King Severin, I demand there be consequences for this attack. If council elders are not to speak plainly for fear of our lives, then everything the Draig believe in will crumble around us. I worry this is the influence of Earth ways. This is what I warned everyone about. Bringing humans through the portal has already begun to change us in more ways than we can cope with."

Lord Montague's statement drew a lot of support from the council.

"Finn?" the queen demanded. "What is the meaning of this display?"

"He insulted my wife," Finn said simply. His frustration worsened. He had no other defense. Technically, what Montague had said about Ivar was true, so that he couldn't call him a liar.

At that, Galina's expression changed from irritation to anger. She took a deep breath. When she spoke, her words were calm—too calm. "Lord Montague, is it true?"

"I only spoke the truth," Montague answered with confidence, giving Finn a superior look as if to say he knew he'd already won this battle. "You saw it for yourself. Princess Sadie allowed herself to be married under a rag. It is a disgrace and further proof that Earth humans are ill-suited to the needs of the dragon. And the prince kept her locked away, avoiding our numerous attempts to contact the human. What other conclusion can be drawn, but that he coached her as to how to answer our questions?"

"That's not true," Finn defended.

"And we are to take your word on this?" Montague snorted with humorless laughter.

"Are you quite finished?" the queen demanded. She didn't wait for an answer. "For it is my turn to speak."

Some of the council members moved back to their chairs. The queen stepped regally into the middle of the room. She waited until everyone had settled in silence.

"When we first looked at opening the portal, I

was not quiet about the humans. Like many of you, I grew up hearing the tales from the old days—horror stories around campfires whispered amongst the men and their sons. It took me a very long time to accept that our dragon sons, *my sons*, would not be marrying dragon-shifters but humans. But as we have come to see, the gods have not given us much choice, and in this, I think the path to our future is clear. We must mend ourselves with our past, so that we may have a future."

Montague looked as if he was bursting to counter her words, but he held back. King Severin merely nodded. Only rarely did the king disagree with his wife. Everyone knew who the ruling force in the royal relationship was. Perhaps that was why female dragons were so scarce. As a singular, a female dragon was strong and fierce, but as a mass, they would be a force to behold.

"Yes, humans are weak and strange," the queen continued.

Montague nodded emphatically. Finn frowned, now fighting his own temptation to interrupt. Kyran gave a small shake of his head, telling Finn to wait.

"As a female dragon, when we brought the first bride through, I worried these humans would lack the strength needed to be one of us. Their skin is soft and delicate. They can't shift to protect themselves. My daughter even walked into a guard shield, nearly taking off her nose when she blistered her face."

Kyran grimaced at the mention of Eve's accident. A few of the council members chuckled behind raised hands. The queen eyed her sons and took a deep breath. Finn furrowed his brow in anticipation of what conclusion she might draw.

"But I underestimated them. Their bodies may be weak, and yes, they will need protecting, but their spirits are resilient." Galina moved her gaze around the room, making sure each man was looking at her. "Princess Sadie stayed in her new home as she prepared herself for her new world. Such changes deserve the proper reflection, and I appreciate Sadie not taking it lightly. As to my son's wedding tent..." The queen arched a brow at Finn. "When I asked the princess about it, she told me that she didn't care where she was married, for she did not care about money and pretty things. She told me she preferred people to jewels, and what was good for the poorest was good for those with wealth. We have all met those gem-studded Nenarraten when they visited." The queen gave a dismissive laugh as she referenced the alien craft that had once landed on Draig land. The pompous females spent all day polishing the stones on their dresses and refusing to so much as feed themselves. "I don't know about you, but Princess Sadie is the kind of woman I want in my family."

Montague's breathing became audible as he was unable to hide back his irritation. The queen's words were swaying his audience, and he didn't like it.

"We respect the council," the king put forth, "but we cannot in good conscience keep our dragon people from their mates. My sons finding their mates on Earth is solid proof that it can be, and will be, done. I have given the request to close the portal a lot of thought and have decided it is to remain open until a more viable option is presented."

This caused some grumbling. Finn took a deep breath, feeling as if he'd won at least one small victory that day.

"However, your concerns are being taken into consideration. There will be tighter regulations on travel," the king assured them. "From now on, we only visit Earth on the one night of darkness each year. This night will be sacred. Those who are lucky enough to find mates will bring them back to where we, the hopeful families, will have marriage tents waiting. Only those who finish a very rigorous training program will be permitted to go to Earth."

"Men must understand that these human brides will need time to adjust to life here," the queen added. "For this reason, there will be no marital relations on the first evening of marriage. After the night in the tent, the women must express their willingness to stay. We are not barbarians. If a bride wishes to leave, we must honor her wishes and trust the gods will guide those who are meant to be here to remain. That is the risk every groom will know going into the portal. It is up to the groom to spend the night convincing his mate to stay."

This caused a strange mixture of laughter and grumbles.

"These human women are to be safeguarded at all costs," the king said.

"I will tell you as I told my sons, as I will tell all our sons when they are to step through that portal and enter into marriage. These women are to be protected. We will repeat it like a mantra until it becomes as much a part of our truth as the dragon itself."

Finn knew what his mother would say next, just as he knew she would not like saying it.

"We must encourage our men to go back to the old ways." It went against all Galina understood to be true as a strong woman, but she wasn't a human woman. Dragons mated for life. If a wife died because she was not equipped to live in a shifter's world, then that dragon would spend possibly hundreds of years alone and in mourning for her.

"Men rule the outside sphere. Women rule the inside sphere," Kyran said, nodding by way of support of his parents.

Finn had to bite his lip. Under his breath, he whispered, "Have you informed Eve of this?"

Kyran chuckled and shook his head in denial, as he answered softly, "By all the dragons' fire, no. And I'm not going to either. My wife will always be her own woman. But let those words calm the elders' fears until humans can prove otherwise."

"Only allowing travel from on the one night of darkness a year?" Montague asked, his voice not as boisterous as before. Though he appeared calm on the outside, his hard gaze revealed otherwise. "Do you admit that Prince Ivar is dead and we're not going back for him?"

"The prince is not dead," Finn stated. "He is his own man, and he made his choice. Anything that transpired between the Var prince and I is a matter between us. When the portals open in a year, I will find him, and I will welcome him back."

"I would say it is a matter that affects us all,"

Montague argued. "This threatens the very fabric of peace between dragon and cat. The fact you cannot see that makes me seriously doubt—"

"We speak with the Var king and queen today," the queen interrupted. Her eyes flashed with golden fire, and the rougher sound of her dragon filled her voice. "Until then, I want to hear no more rumors about any of the princes. If you do not like how we run the kingdom, overthrow us." With that Queen Galina marched from the council hall, declaring, "This meeting is over."

12

"How was the meeting with your brother?" Sadie contemplated the packages laid out on the small table near the kitchen. When the villagers had discovered her interest in trying new foods, they'd been only too happy to supply her with samples from their kitchens and gardens. Some of the dishes she could guess at, but others were a complete mystery. Did she eat them hot or cold, store them in the refrigerator or on the counter? She picked up a fuzzy yellow ball and bit her lip.

What exactly did Qurilixian mold look like?

"The meeting is nothing for you to be worried about," Finn answered.

Something in his voice made her look up from the small gifts. Sadie eyed Finn, getting the distinct impression he was lying to her. She wasn't sure how —maybe it was the tone of his voice, or way his eyes moved away and back, or perhaps the slight furrow of his brow. The sensation was hard to explain, but she knew something was amiss.

"Nothing happened at the meeting?" She asked, watching him closely. In many ways, he was a stranger, but he felt familiar to her.

Sadie felt her chest tighten as if he was pulling a thread from inside her toward him. Her mind focused on that sensation, following it, grasping at where it led like a forgotten word on the tip of her tongue. There was something there, just beyond her thinking.

"I said there is nothing for you to be concerned about," Finn assured her. "What do you have there?"

"Food samples." Sadie was annoyed with the sudden change of subject. It came as she was trying to figure out how she felt about him. The seedlings of her feelings were trying to grow inside of her.

Finn moved toward the table, confused. "Why do you have tiny portions of food?"

"Eve and I were in the village. I mentioned my job was to go around trying different kinds of foods. Some of the locals believed this was a funny occupation to have, but they all began giving me samples of food to try." Sadie smiled. "I thought it was kind of them."

"I am pleased to hear they were kind." Finn nodded in approval. "They accept you as a princess."

"Not all of them." Sadie turned back to the packages. She lifted the fuzzy ball and fingered it. Would it be a sweet explosion in her mouth or a bitter bomb of awful? "One called me a... *gwobr*? I don't know what that is, but it didn't sound like a compliment. Especially when he spat at my feet and followed it with a series of obscene gestures."

Sadie lifted the fuzzy ball to her lips. The sound of Finn's approach made her turn toward him. Her mouth was open and tongue extended to taste the food, so the hard slap to the side of her lips and hand came as a surprise. The fuzzy ball flew from her fingers. Her teeth cut the inside of her mouth.

"Ow, what the fuck?" Sadie placed her hand over her lips to protect herself while cradling the wound.

Finn grabbed the hand over her mouth and pulled her toward the bathroom. "Come! Now!"

Sadie protested, dragging her feet. She had not seen this kind of aggression in him toward her, and it took her by complete surprise. "Finn, what the hell are you doing?"

His breathing became heavy. She grabbed the

doorframe and held tight, resisting. When he looked at her, though, it wasn't with anger it was with panic. He looked as if he wanted to speak, but he couldn't make the words come out. "Now. Wash. Poison."

"Pois...?" Sadie glanced over her shoulder to the food. "Poison!"

She let go of the door frame, surging past him to the bathtub. She dipped her fingers into the warm bathwater while wiping her mouth on her sleeve.

"The seed of the Yellow is poisonous," Finn managed. "Did they give one to Eve?"

Sadie shook her head in denial.

"Good." Finn nodded as if still trying to catch his breath.

"The Yellow?" Sadie couldn't imagine who would want to poison her. She tried to remember who had handed her the seed, but the faces were a blur. There had been a rush of them come to greet her, and many of the names were pronounced in such a fashion she would need more practice to recognize them.

"It is a green plant with a yellow center that grows low to the ground near the Var borderlands. I believe you'd call it a fern. The pollen causes sleep if you inhale it. The seeds are poisonous if consumed. Even children know not to mess with the Yellow."

"I'm not a child," Sadie quipped. His tone irritated her. "How was I to know?"

"I didn't mean that you were a child," Finn dismissed. "You said a man called you a *gwobr*?"

Sadie nodded.

"That is mostly a Var word, and the Yellow grows by the Var borders." Finn took a deep breath. She could see his mind working, but he wasn't forthcoming with his conclusions.

"Are you saying one of the cat-shifters tried to kill me?" Sadie kept her hands in the water and again wiped her mouth on her sleeve. "Does this have something to do with Ivar?"

His expression answered for him.

"They think I'm responsible for Ivar becoming stuck on Earth? Don't they see I am stuck on Qurilixen?"

"Stuck?" Finn repeated. He took a step away from her. His eyes moved to her mouth and then her sleeve. She glanced down to see a small smear of blood where he'd accidentally struck her lips while trying to knock the poison out of her grasp. His hands clutched into fists, and he held them close to his body. "I should not have hurt you."

"It's fine. Thanks for not letting me eat poison."

She remained bent over, her shaking hands immersed in the refreshing natural spring bathtub.

"Those are probably clean." He gestured to the water.

She stood up slowly. Water dripped over her pants, but she didn't care. "I think it's time you told me everything that's going on. I can tell that something happened at that meeting. And someone tried to poison me, and there are apparently rumors that I'm a goblin. I think I have a right to know."

"*Gwobr*," he corrected. "It means witch."

"So much better," she drawled sarcastically. Sadie left the bathroom and moved back toward the food. She didn't touch any of it. What had been the object of her curiosity before, she now avoided like the plague. "If I remember my history lessons correctly, the last time your people lived on Earth witches were being burned alive at the stake."

Finn went to the wardrobe and came back with a piece of parchment. He wrote something down, folded it, and went to the door. He disappeared outside for a few moments before returning without the note. He answered as if he'd never left, "I did not wish to worry you."

"Too late. I'm worried," she said. "Actually, I'm a little terrified. I've had bad food before, but this gives new meaning to what we call on Earth *food poisoning*. What was that note about?"

"I had to report this to the king and queen. We're going to have to stay here until we know it's safe." Finn disappeared into his kitchen and returned with a cloth. He picked up the seed and wrapped it before running his hand over the wall. A small panel opened, and he tossed it inside. Then, systematically, he began clearing the table and throwing the food away. When he'd finished, he took a seat on the couch and eyed her expectantly.

Sadie approached slowly, remembering the last time they'd been on the couch together. Fear and desire were odd companions. Even so, she couldn't help thinking of his mouth against hers, and his hands on her body. Her flesh tingled with anticipation, causing a tinge of need in her stomach.

"They do not blame you for Ivar. They blame me. I think this attack on you was a way to get at me. If the cat-shifters believe that I am responsible for the loss of their prince, they will seek to punish me by hurting you." Finn didn't move to touch her. His eyes turned downward. "As a positive, I think the plan worked. Your being here has convinced my parents to leave the portal open with stricter regulations. It was what was needed. The dragon people will have a chance at a future. And, Ivar being away will ensure the Var support this decision, at least in the short-term."

"And the negative?" she asked.

"The negative?" Finn frowned.

"The downside or, the cons, the bad thing about..." Sadie tried to explain.

"Oh, the cons as in the pros and cons, I remember that from the intergalactic broadcasts Kyran and I watched." For a moment, Finn's expression relayed that he forgot the predicament they were in.

It was enough for Sadie to see a softer, real him.

"You really are a nice guy," Sadie whispered, as she looked at him.

"What?" Finn should have heard her easily, but apparently wanted to make her repeat herself.

"I said you're a nice guy," Sadie said. "I shouldn't have yelled at you. I know you were just trying to save my life."

Her words must have reminded Finn about the serious nature of what had happened. "I promise we will discover who did this and they will be punished. It is a grave offense to try to poison the wife of a prince. The very thought of it makes me ill."

"Why would someone want me dead? I just

arrived here."

"The Draig and Var were already fighting over the portals—cats and dragons who are eager to run through, others who want it caved in, those who leave the planet and do not return, purists who do not like the idea of mating with humans, heretics who think we defy the gods by not sitting back and waiting for women to fall like rain from the sky. Then there are the cats who want freer access and are angry that the portals are on dragon land and under our control. Dragons are angry that cats think they have the right since dragons have had the risk of guarding the portal on our land for centuries. There are so many voices yelling that none of them are heard, so they scream louder and louder and angrier and angrier. I fear this decision will cause yelling to turn into action. Those who do want the portal open will fight it. Those who want to go through will find issue with the regulations. Even the royals and the elders are divided on this." Finn closed his eyes and leaned back on the couch. "And I did not help matters today."

"Finn, what happened at that meeting?" Sadie lightly touched his cheek.

He stiffened as if startled by the contact and looked at her. "I shamed us. I attacked Lord Montague."

Sadie dropped her hand to rest on his chest. His breathing was even under her fingers. She didn't believe for a moment he'd done anything so bad as to cause the forlorn look on his face. "Why did you attack him?"

"He spoke out of turn."

"About?"

"It doesn't matter." He sat forward, forcing her hand to drop away from him. "I should not have lost my temper in the council hall, not with so much at stake. Already rumors about Ivar are out of control. I had hoped we could talk to Gudmund to get them stopped before they spread, but it may be too late. This attack on you only proves tensions are escalating."

"Why Gudmund?"

"We have concluded that he may be the one speaking out of turn," Finn said. His eyes narrowed as he studied her. "Why? Did you feel something when he looked at you?

Sadie frowned and said nothing. She lightly touched her lip.

"What?"

Sadie shrugged. "I don't know. He didn't seem like that type to me. Everything he said and did appear to be in an effort to protect you."

"Only a few knew the details that are now being whispered amongst the people," Finn said. "Someone had to tell them."

"If you say its Gudmund, I'll believe you. I don't know the man and have no reason to persecute or defend him."

"You have no feelings for Gudmund? You are certain?"

Sadie arched a brow. "Why would I? I met him all of two seconds. Honestly, I would have guessed it was that Cleve guy. He appeared a little too eager to be involved. He kept trying to put himself in your eye line like he wanted to be noticed. I've seen it before when people try to get the attention of the commanding officer. He seems like the type who would talk out of turn to anyone of power he'd think would listen. I wouldn't be surprised if he told Montague everything."

Finn stared at her.

"Why are you looking at me like that?" Sadie leaned away.

"Because all of that makes sense." Finn slid to the floor and kneeled before her. His eyes peered into hers, their golden depths pleading before he even opened his mouth. "Lady Sadie, you show great insight into the character of people, and much honor in your words to the queen when she questioned you. Lesser women would have panicked, but you stood up to one of the scariest dragons I have ever met. I have never met a woman like you. I believe the gods sent you to me for a reason."

"Finn, I..." Her breath caught, and she couldn't form words. Emotions welled within her, strong, powerful ones—capable of defying all logic and sense. She believed he was put in her path for a reason.

"I know you have every right to demand a one-way trip back to Earth, and I have no right to deny you. I also have no right to ask this of you, especially after your life was just put at risk, but will you please come with me to meet the Var royal family? Help me explain what happened to their son. Help us avoid a war." Finn walked on his knees until he was next to her. He placed his forehead on her lap. "Please help me save my people, Sadie."

What she felt for him was too real to ignore, and yet he'd been clear that he would never feel the same way.

I am not Finn's true mate.

Each time she thought of the statement, the raw truth hurt worse than the time before.

13

FINN COULDN'T LET GO of Sadie's leg as he gripped her calf. The idea of her leaving caused an ache in his chest that made it hard to breathe. "Please help me save my people, Sadie."

She didn't answer, and he wasn't sure she could hear his muffled words. What right did he have to ask it of her? He'd been a rash fool with Montague, attacking the man as he had. He should have shoved Ivar through the portal when he had the chance. If Finn were trapped on Earth now, none of this would be happening. Ivar would be home. The portals would be open. The letter he'd left would have kept tensions from flaring between the two sides.

Finn worried about Ivar, alone without funds on a planet the cat-shifter was not fond of. He worried about his friend's future. And now, someone had tried to poison Sadie because of his bad choices. The guilt was almost too much to bear.

"I only wanted to save my people," Finn said. "All I have done has been in service to that goal."

Fingers lightly caressed the back of his head, stroking his hair in an understanding manner.

"Perhaps Montague is right about me. I'm impertinent and unfit to rule a kingdom." Finn wasn't sure what caused him to confess as much out loud to Sadie. The embarrassment was hard to admit to even himself. "I am the mischievous prince, rarely taking anything seriously and I ruin everything I touch. I'm not fit to rule."

"Well, like my father used to tell me, if this is the path you are choosing then you're probably right. You had best just give up now and stop making an ass of yourself by trying," Sadie said.

Finn frown and lifted his head. It wasn't exactly the wifely advice he'd been expecting.

"What?" Sadie asked though the word sounded like a question. "You're having a pity party. I will not join you there."

"A pity...?" Finn's frown deepened.

"You thought I'd say something like, it's all going to be fine?"

"Well…" Finn gave a small nod in the affirmative. "Yes."

"Yeah, not going to happen. All that is true, but I won't do you the disservice of helping you wallow and feel sorry for yourself. So what if Montague is a jerk? Nothing we can do about that. Montague is an asshole's asshole. He lives to be miserable, and you know what they say about misery."

Sadie spoke with such confidence. Finn found himself fascinated by the rhythm and flow of their chatter. It didn't matter that he was unaccustomed to her earth dialogue and references.

"No, I don't know what they say about misery," he prompted

"Sorry. I keep on using these awful clichés." Sadie waved a hand in dismissal.

"I liked the way you speak. So, tell me about misery." Finn tried to smile.

"Misery likes company. Monty is angry at everything and wants others to join him in his miserable existence. If you obsess over a few names that some jackass with a god complex called you, then he's right. If you're going to let his words stop you from doing what you must, then he's right. You're not fit to be a leader. And that's fine. Not everyone was meant to be in charge. Some people need to be liked and don't want to make waves, and that works for them." Sadie took a deep breath and reached to hold his face, forcing his eyes to hers. "My advice would be, don't listen to him. You're a great prince. You didn't do anything to deserve his bullying."

Finn didn't move as he gazed into her eyes.

"If you are the prince I suspect you are, then you need to stop feeling sorry for yourself. Where is the man who came to Earth to save his people?"

Finn took a deep breath. "I am here."

"Good. It took courage to jump into a portal, to defy the elders, to plan to stay on a foreign planet with no one to help you. You need to pick yourself up and get ready to fight anyone who stands in the way of your goal. Saving your people. That is what matters. Not Montague. Not what anyone says about you, or what they try to do to me, or anything else. Be the prince. Save the dragon people. Look at all you have accomplished. The portals will remain open. You did what you set out to do."

"You are not angry that I fought Montague in the council hall?"

"Not at all," Sadie said. "I don't encourage physical violence, but if you tell me he deserved it, I believe you."

"*He did,*" Finn thought.

"I believe you," she said. "And as far as Ivar is concerned, I have a feeling he can take care of himself. He'll be just fine on Earth. In a year, we'll go get him."

"*We? Do you mean that?*" he thought.

"Yes, I..." Sadie frowned. She looked at his lips. She jerked away from him, pressing back into the couch. "*What the hell?*"

"You heard that?" Finn asked in amazement. "*You hear me?*"

"*What is going on here?*" she answered, not speaking.

"You chose." He grinned.

"Are you just saying things, or are you in my head?" Sadie tensed. This was not the reaction he expected at such a glorious moment.

"We are in each other's heads," he said. "*Listen, hear me inside of you, let me hear you inside of me.*"

Sadie shot up from the couch in a violent fashion, scrambling over the back of the furniture to land in an awkward pile on the floor. Finn stood over her. She crawled backward, pushing her hands behind her back and her heels into the floor, to get away from him.

"Sadie?"

"Eve said I wouldn't change. Humans don't

change. Why are you in my head?" Her chest rose and fell in deep breaths. Her lips opened and closed, but no sound came out. The connection between them was becoming stronger and her voice inside his mind clearer. *This is too much. I don't want you to hear my thoughts. Get out. Get out. Get out. Get..."*

Finn wasn't sure what to do. The fact she heard him, and he her, meant they were supposed to be together. This changed everything, clarified everything. "Damn my inner, broken dragon. What does that creature know? I should have been listening to my heart all along, Sadie. I knew I felt something when I first saw you. I don't know why it took me this long to realize it."

"It has only been like a week," Sadie mumbled as if confused and trying to make sense out of what was happening.

"I know, I'm sorry. It should not have taken me so long," Finn apologized. "I have no excuse for being so slow to tell you I love you."

"It's only been a week," Sadie repeated. She remained in a strange position on the floor, but at least she stopped crawling away from him. Her breathing eased somewhat.

"I have no reasoning for it, only that guilt over what happened with Ivar kept me from allowing myself to find happiness with you. I hit my head. That could have played a part. Or perhaps I am broken. When I almost died as a child in Crystal Lake, it might have damaged the shifter part of me that would know my mate." Happiness bubbled up inside of him, and he could hardly contain his excitement. He wanted to scream his good fortune from the top of the palace so the whole planet could hear. *"But I know now. You are meant to be my wife. The gods urged Ivar to throw you in after me. They knew what I did not. You are my mate, Sadie, my only wife. I love you."*

Sadie relaxed as she sat forward. Her words were soft and hesitant. "Did you say you love me? I thought you said you couldn't care for me like that. You said..."

"I'm a fool," Finn said. "And you are right. I had to get people like Montague's opinion of me out of my head. I am no longer the mischievous boy running around the countryside. I am a prince, your prince if you will but have me."

Sadie trembled as she stood to her feet. He didn't want her to fear him.

"Sadie, give me your hand." Finn reached for her, stepping around the couch to get to her. She hesitated before lifting her fingers to join his. Finn brought them to his chest, placing them over his heart. "All that I am already belongs to you. Open yourself to me, and you will feel the truth of my words, truths that I cannot adequately explain."

Sadie closed her eyes and took a deep breath. His skin tingled where she touched him. The growing bond was slow to start as if she dipped her toe into the lake to gauge the temperature before diving in. Finn had always been one to act first and think later. It was good that his mate would be the opposite. She would bring him clarity and balance, and he would bring her whatever she desired. Plus, it was good that she wasn't scared to give him a swift kick in the ass when needed.

"I didn't kick your ass," Sadie whispered. "I merely said I wouldn't help you plan your pity party."

"I love you," he said, unable to keep the words in. It was all he could do to watch her lovely face as she tested their bond. He wanted to grab her and swirl her around the room. He wanted to run with her through the halls shouting his good fortune. He wanted to take her to the bed and...

Sadie gasped and opened her eyes. Her gaze darted to the bed as if she'd seen the very carnal image that had popped into his brain. He couldn't help it. He wanted to toss her down to make wild, frenzied, passionate love to her.

The tingling intensified, but he didn't know if it was lust, their growing connection, or the purity of the love he felt. All he knew is that it was all consuming. He loved her. *"I love you."* The words were perfect, and he needed to say them again. "I love you, Sadie."

"I..." She licked her lips.

Pure emotion exploded between them, and in that moment, he felt everything—her fear of almost dying that she suppressed in an effort to be strong, her desire for him, the fear of not knowing her place yet, her doubts about being royalty. He felt her sorrow, sorrow he had caused when he told her he could never love her. That knowledge cut into him deeply. He had never meant to cause her a moment's pain.

Finn tried to pull away, but she grabbed his arm to stop him. She pressed her hand harder against his chest, not that they needed that contact to be connected. "Wait."

Finn closed his eyes and searched deeper. When Finn looked into her, he saw his future—all the possible moments they could have, the kisses, the tears, the laughter. His brother once told him that knowing one's mate was rapturous, but Finn thought that word inadequate to explain what he felt for Sadie. There were no words for this feeling.

He opened his eyes to find her staring at his face. The perfect details of her were clear, too clear. It was then he realized he was shifted into dragon form.

When did this happen?

He honestly didn't know.

"You're worried," Finn said, the dragon made his voice low and raspy, but he didn't shift back. He explored her thoughts as she opened them fully. "You're worried that you will die and I will be left alone."

"Eve said that dragons mate for life and that you live longer than we do. She says that our metabolism is supposed to slow down and we'll live longer on this planet, but there is no proof that is the case. What if I die of old age and you go on for hundreds of years?"

"Then each of those lonely years would be worth it, for I have you now," Finn said. "Do not fear that, Sadie. I don't. None of us knows what the future will bring. But, Eve is right. People do live longer on Qurilixen. The gods would not be so cruel as to let me find my heart, only to take you away too soon."

"You're worried I'll miss Earth," Sadie said. "I will. It's my childhood home. But it is motivation for me to help you keep the portals open so I can visit, and I can still call my mother to say hello. Who knows, maybe one day you will be able to meet her."

"I would like to meet your family," he said.

"It's just my mother. My father passed away a few years ago." Sadie lifted her hand from his chest to lightly touch his shifted face. "*You are amazing. Your eyes are so intense.*"

"I'm glad you're not frightened of me," he said.

Sadie gave a small smile and laughed. "Not frightened. But..." She leaned in to kiss his shifted mouth, not pulling away as she thought toward him, "*but I definitely feel something.*"

Her desire filled him, and he let the dragon armor melt so that he may hold her in human form. "*We are joined. The connection is complete. I belong to you, my love, forever.*"

Her hand snaked down his hips. She pulled her lips away with a small grin. "Well, yes there's that, but I meant another feeling." Her eyes darted meaningfully to the bed and then back to him. "I've been thinking about you ever since I left your bed."

14

Sadie couldn't deny her feelings. The moment he said, "I love you," she had heard her heart whispering it back. Yes, it was fast, but she didn't have to explain herself or this moment to anyone.

She loved Finn. He was her prince. Period.

Finn gave her a small, knowing smile as if he'd heard her inner declaration. Knowing he could read her mind was disconcerting. Even though she didn't feel like keeping secrets from him, it was odd to know she couldn't if she wanted to.

Seeing him shifted, feeling the hardness of his dragon body pressed to hers, had been strangely intimate. His temperature had risen by several degrees, causing her body to heat as well. He looked more medieval dragon than snake-like, though he stood as a man, not an animal—a true man-dragon hybrid. His shifted eyes glowed, moving as if he saw every inch of her and savored it. None of it scared her. She wanted to see it again.

"I cannot take you in dragon form," Finn whispered, as she considered what he looked like shifted.

"That's probably a good thing, but it's not going to stop me from thinking about how sexy my husband is in all forms." Sadie winked. She took his hand and led him toward the bed.

"I like when you call me husband." Finn grinned, clearly not caring that he looked like a besotted fool, and she knew he'd do anything she asked of him. He swooped forward and lifted her into his arms. Spanning the remaining distance, he then laid her on the bed. He tugged eagerly out of his clothing before crawling over her. "And I like calling you my wife."

His lips met hers in an adoring caress. She ran her fingers along his arms to his chest. The strong beat of his heart filled her thoughts with its steady rhythm. The sound only grew louder until she couldn't tell whose heart beat the fiercest.

Finn instinctively read her desires, touching her how she wished to be touched. Their bodies became a frenzy of movements. She tugged to be free of her clothes, wanting contact with his skin. He helped her from her dress before pulling her leggings and underwear off her hips. The strap of her bra dislodged from her shoulder as he kissed the top of her breasts.

Every part of her focused on him. She felt his breath as if it were her own. His mouth met hers, and his hands explored flesh until she was begging him to satisfy her.

The hard length of his arousal brushed up against her thigh and then, finally, glorious pleasure as he entered her. Mindlessly she reached for him, wanting to melt into his body and never leave. This was her forever. She understood that more than she'd understood anything else in her life. Finn was her home. This is where she belonged.

"*I love you,*" his words repeated in her head with each thrust.

The tension built until it became too much to contain. Their bodies exploded in unison. Her climax washed over her. Sadie cried out, only to find his voice joined hers. At first, every muscle in her body tensed before she turned into a pliable, sated mass. He rolled next to her and gathered her into his arms.

"I love you, too," Sadie whispered, not planning on moving from his arms anytime soon.

"Thank you for making me see what I must do.

You were right. I cannot let Monty's words into my head."

"I have to confess, I would have loved to see you hit him in his pompous face," Sadie admitted.

"Can I confess something?" Finn asked, kissing her temple.

"You can tell me anything you like," Sadie answered.

"I'm not sure what pity party means, and I was too afraid to stop you from scolding me to ask," Finn said.

"It doesn't matter now." Sadie rolled onto her side to face him. She stroked the hair from his face. She gave him a small smile. "But don't worry, if I see you having one I'll be sure to step in."

Even as Sadie knew Finn would protect her, she couldn't help the fear that crept over her as the Var king and queen looked her over. Finn stood next to her side, a small comfort as King Severin and Queen Galina flanked their sides. Severin was next to her while Galina chose a place by her son. The council hall stood empty, the ring of chairs and tables encircling the royal families standing in the center of the room. There were no pleasantries, no offers of drinks and comforts. Instead, solemn introductions were met with a telling silence.

Var royals, King Ainmire and Queen Lassairfhina, looked too young to have such serious expressions, but then no one on this planet appeared as old to her as they were. It didn't help that King

Ainmire looked just like his son, so much so that at first, Sadie had gasped in relief and whispered to Finn that Ivar must have found a way home. Though now as she tried not to stare, she realized the king's hair was cut shorter, and he had a scar on his cheek she didn't recall on Ivar—even though her fleeting encounter with the cat-shifting prince had been abrupt and somewhat hostile. She kept her eyes on Ainmire, waiting in anticipation for any sign that fur might sprout and she should run for safety.

Queen Lassairfhina's expression was no less severe. She was a beautiful woman, with generous curves made even more apparent by the dark lines running down her green dress. Her blonde hair was coiled around her head to form a crown. Her eyes did not flash with the golden color of her husband, but Sadie refused to underestimate a woman's love for her missing son. In that way, she couldn't blame them. There had been many nights she'd watched her mother sitting up in worry over her father.

The only kind spot in the Var entourage was Prince Rafe. The cat-shifter men wore shirts with cross laces down the center of their chests with no undershirt as the opening exposed a strip of flesh from stomachs to necks. Though the prince's smile was strained and his eyes tired, he did at least try to smile. The silence became awkward, and Rafe was the one to break it. "I don't think anyone here believes you would intentionally harm Prince Ivar."

"You know I wouldn't," Finn agreed. "I have loved you both like my own brothers since we were boys. I have no reason to want tension between our families."

"Those are not the rumors we hear," King Ainmire stated. His eyes again turned to Sadie. His accent was thick, and she had to concentrate to understand him. "Tell me honestly, m'lady, were you to marry my son?"

An expression that could only be described as hope filtered over Queen Lassairfhina's face at her husband's words. Sadie wasn't sure what to make of it. Did the queen want her son to marry, or did she want a fight with the dragon-shifters?

"I find this line of questioning to my daughter insulting," Galina stated. Another wave of tension rolled over the small gathering, a palpable force that left Sadie feeling a little nauseous.

Sadie tried to think of a diplomatic way of explaining the events. In truth, she had thought she'd merely stand around while everyone else talked and she could just nod or shake her head, whatever the comment called for.

"Do not be afraid," Lassairfhina urged. "Tell us."

"Prince Ivar," Sadie took a deep breath. Her heart pounded. There was so much power—of noble rank and physical abilities—in the council hall, and its undivided attention was all directed at her. Her hands shook, and she could do little to stop them.

"*You are safe,*" Finn's words whispered in her mind. At the intrusion, she gave a little jump of surprise, still not used to talking without talking.

"*Dammit, can everyone hear my thoughts? Is that why they are all looking at me like... peanut butter, pound cake, going shopping, water bottle, water fountain, bubbler, cooler, ice, water, we didn't hurt your son...*"

"*Sadie, relax, you're not mated to them. They can't hear you,*" Finn said.

"*Oh, thank goodness.*" She gave an audible sigh of relief. The sound brought an instant reaction from the Var.

"We're taking this woman under our protection," Ainmire announced.

"Where is my son," Lassairfhina demanded. Her shoulder trembled. "I want my son. The people want their future king."

Sadie glanced at Rafe to see how he would take the comment. He didn't register a reaction.

"My queen, let them speak," Rafe tried to calm his mother. "This is not how we communicate with friends. I am positive we all wish for the same thing here—a resolution and the truth."

"I don't want to be with your son. He frightened me," Sadie blurted. It wasn't the elegant, diplomatic statement she'd hoped or, but it was what came out of her mouth. "He is on Earth."

"You... left... my son... on Earth?" the queen gasped the words as if she couldn't catch her breath. Her hand clutched over her heart. "Alone? On that barbaric planet?"

"Oh, sacred cats, take cover!" Rafe ordered. King Ainmire and Prince Rafe fell to the ground, shifting into cat form before they landed. They covered the backs of their heads with their hands.

Intense heat radiated from the Var Queen. Sadie watched, petrified into place. Three dragon-shifters converged on her, covering her with their limbs and blocking her with their bodies as they forced her to the floor. She caught a glimpse of Queen Lassairfhina on her way down. Red flames ignited on the woman's flesh, shooting fire from her body in all directions. Sadie couldn't help the small scream that leaped from her throat as Finn and his parents created a shield over her with their dragon bodies. A bright light lit up the surrounding shadows. The heat blazed, turning the room into a furnace. As quickly as the threat erupted, it subsided.

The Draig royals were slow to crawl off her. The smell of burnt fibers was prevalent on the air as she turned to look at the Var queen. Lassairfhina stood naked amidst a pile of charred clothing, smoke curling off her skin like a dying campfire. Ainmire and Rafe's clothes had small scorch marks, as did Finn, Severin, and Galina, but their material was mostly intact. Ainmire and Rafe hurried to hide the Var queen's nakedness from view. Rafe tugged off his shirt and handed it to his mother, leaving him only in a pair of tight pants and boots. The Var queen slipped it over her head.

When the men stepped away from Lassairfhina, she was pulling the shirt laces along the front tight to block any view they might give of her nakedness. The attire was nothing compared to the beautiful gown she'd worn moments before. Her body had shrunk as if her explosion had taken most of her bodyweight with it to leave her a tiny fragment of her former self. Luckily, no one appeared seriously injured from the ordeal.

"I apologize," Queen Lassairfhina said. "I'm very upset about my son. I know he would never choose to stay on Earth willingly." She gave Sadie a small glance. "That's not to say your planet is not lovely, my dear, I'm sure it has it's..."

"Pleasantries," King Ainmire supplied when his wife faltered with her compliment.

Lassairfhina nodded. "Pleasantries."

"No one hurt him," Sadie managed, still shaken by what felt to be the second attempt on her life that day. "He stayed there, maybe by accident, maybe on purpose. I can't say. He threw me through after Finn, but he apologized first." She had no idea if her words made any kind of sense, but that was her attempt. "I'm sorry to ask, but what kind of cat are you that lights on fire like that?"

"Sadie," Galina whispered as if scolding one of her children.

"I'm not Var by birth, only marriage." Lassairfhina gestured at her son to bring her a chair. He ran to fetch it for her. "My people are called the Feenik."

"Phoenix?" Sadie repeated. That made sense.

"*Fee-nik*," Lassairfhina sounded out. "I came to this planet with my family." She gave her husband a soft smile. "I met this one and never left. And he gave me two very wonderful sons, and I want them both home." Rafe arrived with the chair, and she lowered herself down with a sigh. "Forgive me. I'm tired. I burned a lot of fuel. You were saying about my Ivar?"

"He's in a good location. The town on the other side of the portal is a respectable one, and people are friendly in the South. I'm sure someone will help him." Sadie glanced at Finn for confirmation.

Finn nodded once. "I found the location to be pleasant."

"And Ivar isn't your mate, is he?" Lassairfhina glanced at Finn and appeared sad. "I can see the answer with my own eyes."

"Even if this was an accident," King Ainmire allowed, "it is ill-timed. The Nutef faction is gaining in numbers, and there have been rumors that Draig members are joining them, which is unheard of since they're mostly cat-shifter purists. I don't know what the spreading news of a missing prince will cause. They do not want humans tainting the royal bloodlines as it is and even tried to sacrifice Princess Jenna. It is why she is not allowed to travel with us."

"I heard about your wife," Finn told Rafe. "I am glad she was not harmed."

"She sends her regards," Rafe answered, before directing his attention toward Sadie. "She's very sorry she couldn't be here to greet you."

"Please, pass along my regret as well. Hopefully,

we can soon rectify that." Sadie took a deep breath before turning her attention to King Ainmire. "The Nutef?"

"They believe in the purity of the shifter. They did not like my marriage to an alien woman," King Ainmire explained, "and they think the Feenik are a noble people. Humans they hate."

"They have made it their mission to sacrifice any human woman we bring through the portals. They believe we will see the resolve of the gods, who do not want tainted Var blood." Rafe added. "Ivar oversaw hunting them down, but it's not easy. Their members include several of the Old House Nobles."

"Our elder council members are not pleased with the portal being open either," Finn said.

"Do you think that is who tried to poison me?" Sadie whispered to Finn.

"You were poisoned?" Rafe asked, indicating her whisper had not been quiet enough. "By who? When? How?"

"There has been an attack on your family?" Ainmire asked Severin. "You did not say."

"It only just happened," Galina put forth. She gestured at Sadie to speak.

"Someone gave me a seed from the Yellow to eat," Sadie said. "I didn't know what it was."

Lassairfhina gasped. "They attempted murder inside the palace walls?"

"I was in the village with Princess Eve. The locals discovered I liked trying new foods, and they were giving me dishes as gifts. One man gave me the seed. I don't remember much about him. I think he had on this brown," she paused and gestured up and down her body, "long, cape-robe kind of thing."

"Another called her a," Finn glanced at his mother almost apologetically, "*gwobr*."

"Brown robes sound like the Nutef," Rafe said, "but poisoning?"

"We have one of our best men looking into it," King Severin assured them.

"Who?" Finn asked.

"Gudmund," Severin answered.

Finn immediately lowered his voice. "I think we should speak after this meeting."

"Your brother and I already spoke about it," Severin dismissed. "Gudmund is as loyal as they come. Already he had supplied us valuable information. I do not expect it will take him long to—"

"This situation is unacceptable," King Ainmire interrupted. "Our princesses are at risk. Ivar was making progress with the Nutef. We thought he was coming to Draig land to investigate the possibility of rebel Draig alliances. Instead of finding the rest to the rebels and securing our future, it turns out he was hopping through the portal with Finn."

"You were investigating on Draig land without informing us?" Galina demanded, her eyes flashing with gold.

"You're using the portal without informing us," Ainmire countered, letting a shift ripple around his eyes. Tiny sprouts of fur appeared briefly. "That was not our agreement. We're supposed to be equal partners."

"Prince Ivar and I went through without telling anyone," Finn interrupted. "He agreed with me that the portal should remain open."

"Perhaps that is why he stayed. To keep it open," Severin offered. "Ivar is a brave man."

"He would not abandon his investigation into the Nutef." Lassairfhina pushed up from the chair. Her son tried to urge her to stay seated, but she swatted his hand away. "He would not go without leaving word."

"He did not plan to stay, but he is there now." Finn tried to sound reasonable. "His last act before the portal closed was to send my bride through. He knows the portal schedule. When it opens, I will be there to greet him."

"As will I," Sadie stated. When they all turned their intense looks in her direction, she added weakly, "for what it's worth."

A long silence fell over the royal families.

"I am not pleased with what you and my son have done," King Ainmire said to Finn. He sighed heavily. "Tensions are already high. This year will not be easy as we wait for Ivar's return—for any of us."

"I have a suggestion," Sadie said, trying not to flinch as they all looked at her again. "What if instead of closing the portals, you let more shifters through? I would think if more of them find happiness and love, then we could dispute the Nutef's arguments about humans being bad. If men truly just want to find mates, as it has been explained to me, then let them. Give them a chance. Send more to Earth. Regulate it. Train them. When morale is low, you must do anything you can to boost it. Do whatever must be done in the background, but hope is your best weapon against fear. Start openly working toward the goal of mass mating, even if you don't send them all through right away."

Ainmire arched a brow. Severin cleared his throat. Sadie bit the inside of her lip, suddenly wishing she could take the words back. They didn't seem to appreciate her thoughts on the matter.

"Hm," Lassairfhina hummed thoughtfully. She nodded her head. "You have married well, Finn. She shows much wisdom."

"She does?" Ainmire glanced at his wife. "But I thought we wanted the portals regulated."

"We want our men to find mates. They're becoming too wild," Lassairfhina countered. "And I want grandsons."

"Yes," Galina agreed, smiling at Sadie. "The gods have truly blessed us."

16

Finn held Sadie in his arms not wanting ever to leave her side. They rested on the bed, even though it was late in the morning and he should be up. He could think of nothing more important than protecting his wife from all outside threats. And if doing so meant laying in her arms all day, well that was a bonus.

"I can't get your mother's face out of my head. She and Queen Lassairfhina both kept looking at my stomach like I'd become pregnant at any moment."

"We will have children when you wish it," Finn answered.

"Don't get me wrong. I do want children. Someday. But it doesn't feel like the right time. There are so many uncertainties and threats happening on this planet right now." Sadie lightly ran her fingers along the side of his face.

Finn smiled at her. The feel of her breath against his neck was amazing. He found himself liking the tender intimacy of the moment—being vulnerable and at her mercy. He had never felt anything like it. He knew this is where he wanted to be. Forever in her arms.

"Do you think Gudmund will figure out who tried to kill me?" Sadie's fingers stopped moving. "Do you think they will try again?"

"I promise to protect you, Sadie." Finn hated to see the fear in her eyes. He knew catching the person who made an attempt on her life wouldn't fix every-thing, but it would be a start to easing those fears. "It looks like you were right about Gudmund. If my father and my wife both trust him, then I trust him."

"They will tell us what they find out as soon as they find it out, won't they?" Sadie insisted.

"Yes, I promise." Finn sat up reluctantly. "I hear someone coming down the hallway now. I should get dressed."

Sadie tilted her head to the side and listened. "Shifter hearing must be amazing. I can't hear anything."

He let the shift flash over his eyes in response.

She seemed to like it when he did that. His voice dipped with sexual meaning. "We shifters are amazing at many things."

"Oh, I'm aware." Sadie chuckled. "Now stop looking at me like that. Get up and get dressed and go save the dragon-shifters from these evil Nutef rebels."

He rolled out of bed, obeying her wishes. He pulled on a plain tunic shirt and pants, pausing long enough to kiss her as she lay on the bed watching him.

"Be careful," Sadie whispered, before adding, *"Don't you dare let anything happen to you."*

"As you command, my wife," he returned just as softly.

Finn's smile lasted until he stepped out of his home into the palace halls. A heaviness came over him. He did not like leaving his wife's side. His love wanted to keep her near. His fear wanted to protect her from all the bad in the world. He wasn't sure what he would do if he lost her. She had become as much a part of him as his dragon. It amazed him the blessings he'd received from the gods in such a short time.

But, then, the cost had been high too. Ivar was trapped on Earth. Sadie's life was threatened. The tensions between the Draig and the Var were mounting.

"*All will be well*," Sadie's voice whispered inside him. "*Don't worry about me. Keep yourself safe.*"

"*Yes, my heart.*" Finn took a deep breath to calm his fears as he heard the footsteps getting closer. As his brother appeared, he asked, "Kyran, is there news?"

"Come. I don't want to talk in the palace halls." Kyran nodded for his brother to follow him. They made their way quickly through the halls. Passing a couple of the palace guards, Kyran ordered, "Stand guard over Princess Sadie."

"Thank you," Finn said.

"Don't thank me yet. If Sadie is anything like Eve, she'll not be happy with the restrictions on her movement." Kyran led him to the portal tunnels.

"Are we going on a trip?" Finn asked.

Kyran held up a hand to his brother for silence. The guards at the portal stairwell entrance nodded in greeting. "Did the king give you instructions?" The guards nodded again. "Good."

When the door closed behind them, leaving them reliant on their shifter hearing and sight to navigate the dark passage, Finn said, "I don't understand. Are the portals going to open up near Ivar?"

"No, not the portals," Kyran whispered. "Gudmund infiltrated a rebel sect."

"What sect?"

"Draig supporters of the Nutef. We were right to suspect him of secrets, only they weren't the kind we feared. Apparently, our parents didn't deem it necessary to inform us of it, but they've had Gudmund spying on several of the others and reporting back directly to them." Kyran passed by the unlit torches, not taking one up as he kept them in the dark. His voice was low as if he worried they'd be overheard. "We couldn't figure out how dragons were sneaking into the portal when it's under lock and key."

"Did you find which guard was letting them through?" Finn paused as his brother ducked under a protrusion.

"Not a guard." Kyran waited for Finn to duck under the same rock. "An old cave system that breaches the tunnel. Someone uncovered it while they were digging out the portal and didn't report it. With the threat against the princesses, Gudmund became more aggressive in his efforts."

"Why didn't the king and queen tell us about Gudmund?" Finn sighed. "We could have helped."

"Because they still treat us like children."

"Me, you mean. They give you responsibilities.

They still see me as a child—some mischievous boy sneaking out of the palace, running around the countryside, and causing trouble." Finn's reputation as a boy was not unearned, but he'd worked hard to show he was worthy of trust.

"Fine, yes, you. What do you expect? From day one you have not taken the portal trips seriously. You have not been looking for a bride. Until Sadie, no one thought you wanted a mate."

"Of course I wanted a mate," Finn countered. "What harm was there in enjoying life while looking? I can be responsible and still have fun."

"Like Crystal Lake when you nearly drowned?" Kyran charged.

"I was a boy. That was decades ago."

"How about the ceffyl races when you were flung off a cliff?"

"Barely a cliff," Finn countered.

"You broke your arm," Kyran said. "That bar fight on Earth."

"Local custom. I was blending in," Finn answered.

"Losing Ivar?"

Finn didn't have an answer for that one.

"I'm sorry. That last one was not fair. I appreciate what you were trying to do, and had I been unmated I might have tried the same thing." Kyran motioned that they should walk. Finn could hardly see his brother's gesture in the darkness. "We should remain on task. The tunnels are this way. Gudmund will meet us there."

Kyran led the way in silence.

About half way through a small tapping noise caught Finn's attention. He saw a tiny thread of light. It was enough to illuminate a waving dragon-shifter hand. He laid his hand on Kyran's shoulders. "There."

"Gudmund," Kyran answered. He quickened his pace and shifted into dragon form before reaching up. Within seconds Gudmund had pulled the prince into a hidden ridge along the top of the tunnel.

Finn darted by several times but failed to see the opening, until Gudmund's hand reached down, triggering Finn to shift before jumping for momentum to help Gudmund lift him into the secret caves. The opening was tight as he passed through. After a short crawl, he was able to stand. Gudmund had lit a torch, making it easier to see.

Kyran stood, peering into a corner. When his brother stepped aside, Finn frowned. Gudmund had Cleve bound and gagged. The man's eyes begged for release, while at the same time conveying he didn't expect the two princes to help him.

"Cleve is the traitor?" Finn balled his hands into fists. He thought of Sadie, of the poison in her hand lifting toward her lips. The urge to beat Cleve into a bloody pile of nothing was temptingly strong. How dare this man betray them? And after they'd given him such an important position guarding the portals.

Gudmund gave a small kick on the bottom of his prisoner's foot. "No, he's merely a fool." He reached down to pull the gag. "Tell them."

Cleve took several gulps of air, pretending as if he needed to catch his breath before speaking, but Finn smelled the young man's fear.

"Go on," Gudmund ordered.

"I thought I was doing right. I believed I was helping our people," Cleve said.

"Enough excuses. Tell them what you have done," Gudmund commanded.

"You weren't letting dragons through the portal," Cleve accused the royals. "Our people are dying out, and you are keeping the cure for yourselves. We all have a right to find mates. That's why I told Montague—"

"Montague?" Finn interrupted. "He is behind the exodus?"

"Why would he send men to Earth? That makes no sense. He wants the portals closed. He hates Earth." Kyran asked.

"No, he doesn't," Cleve denied. He spoke of it with conviction. "He's been sending dragons through to the promised land. He's saving us."

"He's stranding our people on an alien world," Gudmund countered. "He's hurting us."

"What proof do we have that you're telling the truth?" Kyran asked Cleve.

"My word, by my honor," Cleve answered.

Gudmund snorted in disbelief.

Finn pulled his brother away from the two guards so they wouldn't be overheard. "What if Montague started the exodus and the rumors about the portals to cause a fake panic? What better way than to take control and be the hero to the people than by proving you're the only voice of reason in a situation? All those who know the truth would be stuck on Earth when the portal closes."

Kyran shook his head. "What would he have to gain by that?"

"Everything," came an irritated voice.

At the word both brothers lifted their arms, ready to fight. None expected the elder to be in the caves. They had not heard his approach as the sound was dampened by the damp moss along the rocky walls. Montague stood with five men Finn did not recognize—four dragons, and a shifted cat. All six of them were draped in brown robes of the Nutef. They blocked the main entrance to the cave.

"I knew your grandfather. When I was a boy, he was a great ruler," Montague said. "Now there was a man who understood what it meant to be in power. He didn't hesitate to do what must be done. He did not coddle the people. He was a true king."

"Those were different times," Finn said. "Barbaric times."

"And what times are these now?" Montague asked, spreading his arms as he had in the council hall, performing for his robed audience. "Times of weakness and indecision. A time of weak princes who don't know their place," he motioned to Finn, and then Kyran, "and future kings who can't control their own brother."

"My brother does not need to be controlled," Kyran spat. "You do."

Montague laughed, holding his stomach and tilting back his head. "He abandoned the Var prince. His actions threaten war upon our people."

"War?" Finn repeated. He sized up the robed men. Even with Gudmund, they were outnumbered two to one. "No one is speaking of war. We met with the Var royals. They know Ivar chose his own actions."

A few of the men glanced at each other as if silently questioning the truth of Finn's words.

"If the Var royals rule their kingdom as loosely as you do yours, then I doubt they can control their people any better than you have. The Draig need strength, not weakness. We need leaders," as he spoke, Montague's eyes moved to Cleve, "not friends."

"I only spoke the truth. We are—" Cleve tried to explain.

"Quiet. You betrayed your brothers," Montague warned the bound man.

"Careful, my lord," Gudmund warned. "What you speak of borders on treachery."

"I'm sorry," Montague laughed, the boisterous sound annoying in its loudness. He held out his hand, and one of his followers placed a knife in it. "Borders on?" The blade moved leisurely in the air. "I thought I was clearer than that. We want to overthrow the monarchy. We want strength in the throne of power. We want—"

"By all the dragons, stop blustering," Finn said in

exasperation. "I'm tired of hearing that you want to be king. We get it, Monty."

Montague's face turned red with anger at the impudent tone. The odds were not great, seven Nutefs against the three of them.

"It will not happen," Kyran stated.

Montague shifted and leaped forward, hoping to get the upper hand. Finn's dragon armor covered his body in defense but not soon enough. He felt the deep cut of a talon down his arm. It ripped his flesh, leaving it burning. He threw his hands up, knocking Montague's hand that wielded the blade. The elder released the knife, and Finn heard a sickening thud as it found a target.

"Kyran?" Finn glanced back. His brother was unharmed. The blade had imbedded in Cleve's side. When he turned back, he caught the gleam of satisfaction in Montague's expression that the blade hit the target it did. Cleve groaned softly but was helpless in his binds.

At the elder's actions, four of his robed followers backed away, staring at Cleve in disbelief. They ran from the cavern, evening the odds. The other two attacked. The room became a flurry of swinging limbs and slashing talons. Finn reacted on instinct, blocking assaults as they came. His heart beat hard, pumping energy through his entire body. He thought of Sadie, of protecting Sadie. These men had tried to kill her.

He saw Kyran and Gudmund at his side, calling out commands and warnings, answering those Finn shouted in return. The Var's fur came out in clumps in his hand. The cat-shifter must have thought better of the confrontation because he pulled away, running from the dragon battle after the first wave of cowards.

Finn faced Montague with his brother. The elder's face lost all bravado as he realized Gudmund had forced his only remaining ally to the ground and he faced two angry princes. Never in his life had he remembered fear crossing over those old features. He lifted his hand as if that would stop whatever fate awaited him.

"Finn, it is your wife he tried to have killed," Kyran said. "What do you want to do with him?"

Finn wanted to kill the elder, but he thought of Sadie. What would Sadie want? She'd told him that she didn't approve of physical violence. Would she approve of this?

"Justice," Finn grunted, barely able to get the word out past his heaving breaths. The shift distorted his voice, making it sound angry.

"You can't do that," Montague cried in a last

determined effort. "I am the head of the elder council. You—"

Kyran lifted his hand, ready to strike at Finn's command. The elder recoiled in fear.

"No," Finn grabbed his brother's hand. "Death is too kind. Let's take him back to the palace. Let him face his crimes."

"What about Cleve?" Gudmund asked.

"He's dead," Finn answered, unable to hear the man's breathing. "There is nothing we could have done."

"Then we add murder to the charges," Kyran stated.

"Murder?" Montague spat. "Of a traitor?"

Finn arched a brow at the irony of Montague calling someone else a traitor.

"You won't get away with this," Montague continued, breathing easier as if he realized the princes would not be killing him.

Finn could listen to the man no more. He swung his fist into Montague's jaw, knocking him unconscious.

"I couldn't have said it better myself," Kyran stated.

17

Sadie pressed close to Finn's side as they watched Gudmund force Lord Montague to his knees before King Severin and Queen Galina. The Var royals stood to the side, keeping silent as they watched events unfold. Standing in the back of the room were several elders called to the private hearing to bear witness. Sadie felt their eyes on her but didn't look in their direction.

"Lord Montague," Finn stated, "you have attempted murder on a princess, and murdered the portal guard, Cleve. You have sent our dragon-shifter brothers through the portal under false hopes and abandoned them to an uncertain fate. You have lied to the council of elders and to the royal Draig and Var families. You spread rumors and deceit." Finn lightly gestured to his bloody arm. "You attacked Prince Kyran, the future king, and myself. You have hidden the location of a secret cave that gave access to the Earth portals. You—"

"I reject your claims and should not have to be subjected to them," Montague interrupted. As the man spoke words she didn't understand, Finn translated them for her using the link between their minds. "Untie me at once. I am the head of the elder council. This injustice is uncalled for."

"On my word, my claims are true," Finn stated.

"Like anyone can take the word of someone like you," Montague spat. "I apologize, my king and queen, but I must defend my honor. I have been a loyal Draig subject and have spent my years dedicated to the elder council. Prince Finn is a nuisance who cannot be taken at his word. He is more absorbed with his own amusements than the greater good and the future of the kingdom. Who could take his word over mine?"

"I would," Sadie said softly.

Montague scowled at her.

"I would," Kyran answered. "I know these charges to be true."

"I would take the word of my son," King Severin said.

"Of course, you would," Montague spat. "He's your son."

"I would," Queen Galina answered.

"I would," Prince Rafe added.

"As would I," Queen Lassairfhina said. Sadie glanced at the elders. The Var queen's words appeared to sway them, as it was her son trapped on Earth.

"And I," King Ainmire agreed.

"I believe Prince Finn," one of the elders stated. Montague turned to glare at the man. Sadie didn't know who he was, but she nodded gratefully at him. "Lord Montague has brought shame to the council."

"Princess Sadie," Queen Galina stated. Sadie was ready to be called upon. "As the highest-ranking member who has been aggrieved by Lord Montague directly when he ordered your assassination, we leave it up to you to suggest his fate."

"I..." Sadie looked at the elder. His eyes were hard. No part of him appeared sorry for what he'd done. She felt Finn's arm tighten around her.

"*Whatever you think is just,*" Finn said so only she could hear. "*We trust you.*"

"I would suggest death, dungeon, or exile to Earth. His choice. Death as he wanted to offer me. Dungeon, because he cannot be allowed to roam this planet, at least not until the threat he caused has subsided. But, he'll live. Or, Earth, where he sent many to their fates with his lies. He'll have no reason to kill on Earth, and no power to influence others. We will give him supplies to support himself."

"No. That's not—" Montague tried to argue.

"A very fair judgement," Queen Galina interrupted.

"*Well done, my love,*" Finn directed at her.

"Choose," King Severin ordered. "Death, dungeon, or exile?"

Montague looked around, but no one came to his aid. Finally, he said, "Exile. I am disgusted by this atrocity of—"

The Draig king clapped his hands loudly, stopping the man's words. "Gudmund, take him to the prison. We will find a suitable place to send him, far away from human societies."

Loud murmurings rose over the council hall. Sadie faced her husband and rested her forehead on Finn's chest. "Can we please go home?"

"Of course," Finn agreed. He spoke to his parents, and the visiting royals, before escorting her from the hall.

Sadie breathed a sigh of relief. "I'm glad that's over."

"As are we all," Finn said. "I always knew Monty was a shady character—*that is what you call them, right?*—but I would have never guessed the full extent of his maneuvering."

Sadie reached for his arm. The sleeve was bloody, but the wound beneath had been bandaged.

"I promise, it is fine," he said, not for the first time.

"I know, but the idea of you being injured, or worse, it just..." Sadie couldn't even finish the thought.

"Shh, my sweet *fea*, don't you realize? After everything we've faced so far, the gods have blessed us. We're fate. We're forever."

"I love you, Finn." She leaned up to kiss him, not caring that they were in the palace hall where anyone could walk by. "*We are forever.*"

18

"WHAT IS that light on the fireplace?" Sadie yawned and narrowed her eyes as if that would help her see in the darkness. The top curtains were drawn, and the fire had gone out. She lay on the couch with her husband, having fallen asleep pressed against his naked body.

"What light?" Finn asked, evidently not opening his eyes to look.

She craned her neck to look at his face. Using their psychic link, she said, *"Hey, dragon-shifter, use that super eyesight of yours."*

He opened one eye. It was already shifted, but he looked at her instead of the fireplace. "As my wife commands."

"Seriously, what is that?" She kissed his chin before turning her attention back to the mantle.

"Huh." Finn's arm slipped from behind her head. "I don't know. It's coming from my childhood treasure box."

Sadie tucked her arm over her head and watched his naked ass as he walked away. The man definitely had no shame when it came to being without clothes. Why should he? He was the most gorgeous creature she'd ever seen. And he was all hers.

Finn returned to the couch and nudged her foot with his leg so she would make room for him to sit next to her. She rolled up and draped her arm over his shoulders, resting her head against him to watch as he slowly opened the box. The soft glow from within came from an object at the bottom. Finn dug his fingers into the treasures and pulled out a small necklace.

"What is that?" she asked, leaning closer to see.

"It is the crystal that I retrieved from the bottom of the lake when I almost drowned as a boy. It has never done this before."

"Let me see." Sadie reached for the crystal and as her hand neared the glow became stronger. The object almost seemed to pulse with its own energy and life. As their fingers touched, she felt him, their connection deepening further. The pulsing became stronger. "What's it doing?"

"I'm not sure. I used to wear this as a good luck charm. Not once did it ever give a hint of light." He kept his hand on hers as they watch the pulsing crystal.

Sadie lifted her other hand to his chest. The crystal pulsed in time with the beat of his heart. Then she felt her heart, and it too matched the stone. "I think it's connected to us somehow."

A loud knock sounded on the door. "Finn!" It was Kyran.

Sadie gasped, and the crystal slid from her fingers. It landed on the hard floor, cracking on impact. A wave of intensity washed over her making it hard to breathe.

Kyran knocked again.

"Busy," Finn called, not answering the door. Kyran responded in the Draig language, to which Finn yelled, "Fine."

"What is it?" Sadie asked. She'd only been able to pick up a few of the words.

"Var royals. Council hall. One hour." Finn stared at the floor. "They will want to discuss my going through the portal to find Ivar."

"I'm going with you," Sadie stated.

"Of course, my love, as you wish." He still stared at the ground.

"I'm sorry, Finn, I didn't mean to break your good luck charm. Maybe I can fix it?" Sadie reached for the broken necklace.

Finn stopped her. "*I did not think it possible, but our connection is stronger.*"

Sadie did feel it. It surged through her cementing what she already knew that his life was intertwined forever to his. "Magic?"

"The will of the gods," Finn said. "I feel it deeply. When I nearly died, something must have happened. My dragon broke, and that part of me became infused into the stone. Now, the crystal breaks and I am made complete again. Or, perhaps carrying it around my whole life soaked in part of my power."

"So you're not mad I broke your crystal?"

Finn grinned. "How could I ever be mad at you, my love? What are stones and trinkets to what we have?"

"You do say the sweetest things," Sadie whispered, drawing her around his neck to pull him into her kiss.

"By my estimate, we have about forty minutes

before we have to run to the council hall." His hands slid down her hips to pull her onto his lap.

Sadie chuckled. "Fifty if we show up fashionably late."

"The kings and queens won't like that," Finn warned, though he hardly looked worried.

"They'll be fine," Sadie said. "We'll just tell them we were trying for a baby."

Finn moaned in approval as his kiss deepened. Suddenly, he pulled back. "When we have a son, I know what I'm going to do. I'm going to go down to Crystal Lake and get him his own stone. That way, he may have the luck his dad had in finding his mate."

"Don't you think you're getting a little ahead of yourself?" Sadie questioned.

Finn flipped her onto her back in one swift movement. He pushed her hair from her face and gazed into her eyes. "No, my love. I want everyone to feel the way I feel in this moment. My heart is full, and it is all for you."

"*I love you,*" she answered with her mind as he cut off her words with a kiss. "*Forever.*"

The End

Captured by a Dragon-Shifter Book Six

He's a cat-shifting prince from another planet. She's a human who says she's not interested in an Alpha boyfriend. When they meet there's an undeniable attraction, but is simple chemistry enough to over-come intergalactic odds?

Find out if this Headstrong Prince can win his princess.

New York Times & *USA TODAY*
Bestselling Author

Michelle loves to travel and try new things, whether it's a paranormal investigation of an old Vaudeville Theatre or climbing Mayan temples in Belize. She believes life is an adventure fueled by copious amounts of coffee.

Newly relocated to the American South, Michelle is involved in various film and documentary projects with her talented director husband. She is mom to a fantastic artist. And she's managed by a dog and cat who make sure she's meeting her deadlines.

For the most part she can be found wearing pajama pants and working in her office. There may or may not be dancing. It's all part of the creative process.

**Come say hello! Michelle loves talking
with readers on social media!**

www.MichellePillow.com

facebook.com/AuthorMichellePillow

x.com/michellepillow

instagram.com/michellempillow

bookbub.com/authors/michelle-m-pillow

goodreads.com/Michelle_Pillow

amazon.com/author/michellepillow

youtube.com/michellepillow

pinterest.com/michellepillow

"Hotty Toddy!" The aggressive battle cry rang out over the plaza, a second time.

Prince Ivar of the Var immediately tensed as his urge to shift became almost insuppressible. Around him, the natives gravitated toward the man on the balcony who in turn grinned in pride at the frenzy he'd created. "Hotty Toddy!" The noise carried, echoing through the streets.

Hotty Toddy was not an exclamation Ivar had heard before. Not on his home planet of Qurilixen, at least. Actually, very little about this place reminded him of home.

Ivar's senses continued to tingle. On edge and defensive, he turned slowly, putting his back to Prince Finn of the Draig. His shifter hearing focused on the distance for any signs of trouble. He was aware of what humans thought of alien visitors from the movies he'd seen in Earth theaters. The princes were alone. There was no one to help fight off an attack. If planet officials suspected who they were, it could end badly, and they would have to make a run for the secret portal that would take them home.

The battle cry finally dissipated and nothing more happened.

"We should leave." Ivar turned his attention toward the balcony.

The commander stood next to a dining table watching them. He was not dressed as warriors on Ivar's home world, but he clearly had authority. His cheeks were flushed as if he'd been drinking, never a good thing when a man was in charge of others.

Ivar reminded himself that he had acted in error and deserved the human reprimand. He had not meant to scare the fragile human child in a pink dress as she pranced across the painted lines on the street, but the girl had tried to grab one of the cross laces holding the sides of his shirt closed. Of course he'd growled at her. She should not have touched him. He glanced back, seeing the father consoling the frightened girl.

As a cat-shifter, Ivar could either half shift or

fully shift into the form of a tiger. If he needed to disrobe quickly, he could, which is why there were cross laces along the sides of his pants and shirt. He did not wish to undress on a public human street.

"That man must be a commander." Ivar nodded toward the general on the balcony. He wore a white shirt with large blue flowers on it and short pants. He held a brown bottle in his hand and took frequent drinks from it. "See how he stands above the others surveying the area from a vantage point?"

"I don't think that was a threat," Finn corrected, clearly more curious than worried about this unexplored location. "I see no one coming for us."

Finn was Ivar's only traveling companion on this journey. When the dragon-shifter approached him with the idea to sneak onto Earth without permission from their royal parents, Ivar should have said no. He should say no now and demand they go back before anyone noticed they had left.

If anything happened, their people would not realize they were gone until it was too late and the portal, their only way home, had closed. As much as he liked Finn, Ivar knew the dragon prince was not known for being responsible. It would be up to Ivar to make sure they both made it back home safely.

"Still, perhaps we should show respect to the

local Earth authorities." Ivar turned toward the balcony, placed a fist over his heart, and then bowed, urging Finn to do the same.

The commander laughed and pointed down at them before pushing to his feet and bowing in return.

"Let us retreat to another section of this town, away from that man's sight." Ivar's words were more of a command than a suggestion. He didn't wait for Finn to answer before he started to walk.

Yes, Finn was also a prince, and their sneaking through the portal to *Miss-is-sip-pie* had been his idea, but the man was not the ideal leader for an expedition of this importance. Dragon-shifters were usually more disciplined than Finn.

Conversely, Ivar was told that he had a particular drive and discipline which was unnatural for cat-shifters. Headstrong is what his mother called it, which was a much kinder word than what Ivar's brother, Rafe, used.

Finn was too enamored with the Earth people to make wise decisions. He spoke of humans like they were simply shifters who could not shift, with a naiveté and vulnerability that made them even more fascinating to behold. Earthlings were like children in the universe, unaware of anything beyond their home. Earth was not the only planet, and humans were not the only alien race nor did they represent the only way to live. Aliens had yet to make first contact with them, and humans still lived securely in the belief that everything centered around them and their needs.

Besides, Finn rarely took anything seriously, which is why his coming to Ivar with this plan had been such a surprise. Out of all the princes, Finn never acted like he *wanted* to find a wife. Trips to Earth had been a chance to get into trouble and have adventures away from the prying eyes of their parents and the rest of shifter nobility.

This trip was different. The plan was to find wives, *any wives*, and bring the women home before anyone knew the princes were missing. If they could prove they had been well matched by the gods with human women, they could convince the assembly of elders to keep the portals open.

And that is where things became tricky. To obtain ultimate happiness, a shifter needed to find his true mate. Tonight, they were taking *any* mate. They would be married to women who were not their true mates, obligated to pretend they had found their destinies. In doing so, they would save the future of their people. The princes would be forever joined in this secret that they'd be forced to carry.

Ivar never thought Finn would have it in him to make a sacrifice that put his people before himself. If this night went as planned, Ivar's opinion of the dragon-shifter would be forever changed.

The Earth town looked familiar insomuch that it was alien constructed and appeared like the ones his people had seen on the transmission waves caught on his home world. No, Earth people called it television, not transmissions.

The structures were not like those on Ivar's planet. They were fat and square and squished together. The area centered on a large white building encircled by a road as if to mark its importance by forcing vehicles to drive around it. Across the street on all sides from the showcased building, other structures pressed tightly together with balconies above the walkway, as if to keep those humans below from looking too far past the wares and foods being sold. There was no distant landscape, no fields and forests.

When the shifters had first started coming to Earth, they tried to blend in with the locals. Ivar had told women he was a drag queen, which he quickly found out wasn't the best way to secure a bride. His people thought it meant royalty. It also turned out that Earth was diverse and had enough strange fashions and rituals that their native garb barely drew attention.

Whereas Ivar dressed like a Var, Finn wore a looser tunic style shirt over dark pants and boots common to dragon-shifters. Dragons only half shifted into what looked to be a man-dragon hybrid and did not need to strip out of their clothing. They both carried bags against their hip with thick straps across their chests. Each filled with Earth cash-money, and food rations in case they did not find anything suitable to eat.

Ivar did not want to be on Earth long. Everything about the planet made him uncomfortable. He looked around, hoping to see a woman he could take home to be his wife. It shouldn't be too hard to find a female willing to be a princess, even if it was on an alien world.

Ivar would not be the one to introduce humans to the truth of the universe. The prince simply wanted to find a mate. He would then take her through the portal to his home world to live in the Var palace, and they would never visit this primitive planet ever again.

Surely the gods would bless him this time. He did his duty. He took care of his family and his people. He'd begged them to bless him. He did every-thing he was supposed to do.

If the gods were with them, they'd find their true mates and be home before an hour had passed. He glanced over the crowds, suspiciously watching the locals. The swish of a white skirt caught his attention as a woman disappeared around a corner. He had the urge to follow her but stopped himself.

Who was he kidding? He wasn't sure the will of the gods could be heard in a place full of so much noise and clutter.

There were no women appropriate for mating that he could see. He'd thought the shifter scouts had marked this location as unusable because of the semi-public location of the portal opening when it materi-alized. In fact, it might have been because every female he could see was either too young or appeared to be wearing a marriage finger shackle.

Ivar thought of his younger brother. Rafe's wife, Jenna, came from Earth and the two of them had a stable union. They'd met in a place where humans procured food. If his brother's happiness were any indication, such a meeting place would be lucky.

Finn's brother had found his wife in a tavern. Eve had been on a stage singing bizarre words. She'd also been drunk. Ivar would never question the will of the gods, and they chose Eve to be a princess, but he had come to the conclusion that most tavern women were not looking for mates. Ivar liked Eve well enough but did not want such a handful for his bride.

"You're quieter than usual," Finn said, as they moved down the sidewalk away from the town center. The further they walked, the fewer people they saw. Buildings turned into large houses that were set back from the street. "Are you having second thoughts about our mission?"

"No," Ivar said without hesitation. "I was thinking that I do not understand why those dragons would choose to defect through the portal to live here permanently."

Ivar instantly wished he wouldn't have broached the subject.

Finn frowned. "One problem at a time. If we keep the portals open, I plan to find the lost dragons and bring them home. I think I have narrowed down which location they have been using. It is a place called New Orleans. I honestly believe the only reason they left our world was to find brides. I cannot blame them for that. By going through with our plan to prove happiness in marriage is possible, and to regulate travel, we can end future defection."

"New Orleans? I am not sure I have been to that portal stop," Ivar said.

"My brother has been there with his wife. When Eve was kidnapped by a cat-shifter from the Nutef faction and brought there to die, Kyran went after her. I have traced the time when the dragon-shifters left, and it seems to point to that location. We have extra guards assigned to prevent future problems. If I can get them to come home, it will calm many of the fears and rumors about Earth."

Ivar didn't speak.

"I know this was my idea, and I'll understand if *you* change *your* mind," Finn said.

"I will not change my mind." Ivar again did not hesitate. He knew what needed to be done. "I don't like the idea of taking women against their will, but I have not changed my mind."

"Kidnapped brides are not what either of us wants, and I pray it will never come to that. I keep asking myself, what if the women don't want to be married, or if they make us miserable? What if they are unkind or driven by vanity and ego?"

As much as he didn't like Finn's impetuous attitude, seeing him worried was almost worse. "Then we will have to smile, and lie, and pretend to love our wives for the rest of our hundreds of years. We agreed, and I do not wish to change my course. You were right. This is the only way to force the elders to keep the portals open. Without brides, our people die out. This will be the secret we carry to our graves. It is a sacrifice we must be willing to make."

"I don't think Lord Montague will ever be convinced to keep the portals open," Finn said. Lord Montague was not only a dragon elder but also the stoic leader of the dragon council of elders. He was the most outspoken when it came to closing portal travel forever.

"If you convince the other elders, then there's nothing he can do to stop it." Ivar had never seen Lord Montague with anything but a look of disapproval and disgust on his face. He doubted the man liked anything.

They had snuck through the portal for a reason and could not lose sight of that goal. Tonight was not about love. The odds of the gods blessing them were not great. They'd tried so many times before with no luck. Yes, they hoped to find their true mates, but if that didn't happen—one way or another—they would be leaving with women.

The plan was to defy tradition and create their own blessing. They would take half mates, ensure the future of the shifter population, and never let a moment of discontentment show.

Cat-shifters had taken half mates in the past, but those were marriages of convenience. Ivar wanted a love like his parents had, like his brother had, but this wasn't about his wants. He was a prince. He had a duty to his people as did Finn. What mattered more? The fates of two princes? Or the survival of thousands?

"I keep hoping women will walk up to us and say, 'The gods sent us to you. We are your true mates. Take us home and prove to the elders that human women make viable wives and the portal should be left open so that others may come and be happy.' But I know that is unlikely," Finn said.

"If only it were that easy." Ivar agreed the fantasy had appeal, but he did not want to be drawn into fanciful daydreams. "We should not place our bets on such horrible odds."

A young man walked past them and gave them a strange look.

"We should use the Earth language." Ivar hadn't realized they'd slipped into their native tongue. They initially had learned to speak the Earth languages from the television transmission waves floating around space and then furthered their vocabulary as those first scouts came to investigate the portal openings.

"Like our talking about the decreasing population of dragon-shifters and cat-shifters due to a lack of females would draw less attention than our foreign words." Finn laughed. "Maybe we should announce ourselves. Perhaps the women would line up to marry us."

"I'm glad you find amusement in this." Ivar's tone expressed the opposite. He wasn't glad. Not about any of this. He couldn't help the sternness in his voice. The future of his people was not a game.

"I'm sorry, Ivar. I do not mean to make light. I know you do not want to be on this planet. You have made that clear on every trip to Earth we have taken." Finn took a deep breath. "I don't want to do this either. I want a wife, but not like this."

"There is nothing down this road but houses and traffic," Finn said. "We should turn around."

"Agreed. We do not want to wander too far from the portal." Ivar followed Finn's lead, and they moved in the other direction. "We will stay close to that central location where there are many gathering places and hope that more women appear."

They quickened their pace to hurry back toward the center of town. Turning down a small inlet with tables, they heard people talking. Children screamed, running with their hands in the air as they carried colorful ice cream cones.

Ivar lifted his hands wide to the side. "I did nothing this time to make them scream. I didn't even look at them."

"I think that sound is excitement, not fear," Finn said.

"You have to come back here for a football game this fall," a boisterous voice demanded. They turned to watch the commander from the balcony pass by the inlet. "We might not win all the games, but we never lose a party. The fun starts at the tailgating and doesn't end until dawn."

"I think ol' Donald here secretly works for the tourist board," one of the commander's men teased. The group walked on, and Ivar let go of his captured breath. He did not want to be blamed for frightening more children.

"What is football?" Finn asked.

Ivar gestured that he did not know.

"Perhaps we will have better luck if we take different paths," Finn suggested. "We do not have much time, and we can cover more ground apart."

Ivar nodded. "The sound does carry here. Stay within shouting distance to the center. If that portal closes, we're trapped for a year until it reopens. We both need to be gone before that happens."

Finn's expression turned unusually serious as he looked around. "No. Of course we wouldn't want that."

"The commander has left." For some reason, Ivar was drawn to where he'd seen the woman in the white skirt. Perhaps if he followed in that direction, there would be more women. "I'll head back the way we came. You can explore here. If either of us finds suitable brides, we will meet in the middle."

"A fine plan," Finn agreed.

Before the man could leave Ivar placed a hand on his arm to stop him. He wanted to say something comforting, but there were no words. "We have to believe that kindness in a mate will be enough and that happiness can be found in duty."

Finn didn't answer.

Ivar had seen the look on his brother's face each time Jenna entered the room. He saw their love, their devotion, and their contentment. As pleased as he was for Rafe, their happiness over the last few years had made Ivar's loneliness worse.

"We will not have that mad rush of passion that others talk about," Ivar continued, "but in the end, our pleasure will have to come from seeing others find mates. If that is the sacrifice the gods demand, then we will pay it."

"Yes. We will pay it." Finn nodded sadly.

Before Ivar could say anything more, Finn took off through the inlet in the same direction the children had come from.

Ivar wondered if the dragon prince was reconsidering their decision. He couldn't say it would surprise him. When the time came to decide, he wasn't sure how Finn would act.

Read the whole story, Captured by a Dragon-Shifter: Headstrong Prince in stores now!

COMPLIMENTARY EXCERPTS

255

PERFECT PRINCE

BY MICHELLE M. PILLOW

Want more Draig?

Dragon Lords Series

A Perfect Escape...

Nadja Aleksander has everything she could ever want in life, except her freedom. Skipping out on her engagement, to a man her controlling father has chosen for her, Nadja books passage on the first spaceship she can find. Bound for a planet of primitive humanoid males, Nadja plans on finding a simple, hardworking man who will allow her to live out her days in total obscurity.

A Perfect Mistake...

Dragon-shifter Prince Olek is pleased with his refined and blushing bride. When she chooses him to be her life mate, appearing happy in her decision, his heart soars—until the next morning when his new princess wants nothing to do with him. Olek doesn't know what he's done to upset his alluring bride, but he is determined to reignite the hot sparks that burned the night they met.

Perfect Prince Excerpt

"Come, bride."

Again, she couldn't deny him, moving to dip under the green tent flap he held up for her. When she drew near him, she smelled the warm oil on his glistening skin. It mixed with the natural scent of him. She breathed deeply. This was as close as she had ever been to such an inadequately dressed man before.

She faltered in her movements, glancing up into his eyes. Before she knew what was happening, a strong hand was on her face, gently cupping her cheek. The touch was fire to her already flushed features. Her lips parted with a ragged, scared gasp.

Olek took it as an invitation and dipped his head forward.

Nadja almost screamed when he tried to kiss her. Her first reaction was to run. Dodging under his arm, she darted inside the tent. Nadja froze mid-step as she looked around. The red earth floor was covered completely in soft furs. It cushioned her feet beneath her slippers. Below the center point of the pyramid was a high platform bed, which required a step to climb onto it. Silk hung down around the sides, stirring delicately in the torchlight like soft white clouds.

She should have run *out* of the tent, not in.

Spinning to do just that, she realized the only exit was still blocked. She was trapped. Olek grinned, though the look seemed baffled.

"I-I," she stuttered, not sure how to explain her rude behavior, or if she even should.

Olek let the flap fall shut behind him as he followed her inside. He resembled a stalking beast after his prey, relishing the anticipation of the hunt.

Nadja turned from him and was again met with the giant bed. She recoiled from it as if it was covered in poison. It occurred to her how intimate this night really could be. Stumbling back, she bumped into an incredibly hard chest.

She jolted in panic, scurrying away from the

solid, warm muscles. Her eyes darted around, taking in the three corners of the enclosure. In the first, there was a bath drawn, the steaming water coming out of the basin. A sweet perfumed scent rose with it. Folded towels, bath oils, and rinses were neatly arranged at the side.

The next corner had a table full of chocolates, fruits and cream sauces. A bench with cushioned seats stretched along the side, resembling a couch. An earthen wine jug was set in the center. Feeling the heady consequences of the liquor she had drunk too much of at the feast, she turned away from the food.

The third corner, behind the bed, was harder to see from her position so she ignored it. Feeling rather than hearing Olek coming up behind her, she again panicked. Swirling to face him, she held up her arms and backed away. Her hands shook. This was not how she imagined being alone with a man would feel like. She always assumed it would be like reporting to one of the robot guards, or talking to a dignitary at some function she was forced to attend.

But Olek was half naked and smiling at her like he knew every thought in her head. Did he somehow realize she liked looking at his oiled chest, to the point where she made a conscious effort not to? Could he know that when his hand had briefly held hers, her nerves had tingled, were still tingling? That the idea of his kisses both excited and terrified her?

Merriment poured from his gaze and she blushed to see it. He held back, standing tall as Nadja studied him. Before she realized it, her eyes were traveling a seductive journey of discovery over his taut chest. Already his small nipples were hard buds. His flesh dipped in all the right places only to rise and swell with each of his shallow breaths. There was no fat on his chiseled form and she doubted they employed beauty services to remove fat cells on a planet like this. His body was all natural. She bit her bottom lip, absently chewing at it as she looked him over.

His broad shoulders carried his strong arms with ease. They were arms that could crush her if he so chose. The metal band on his biceps would have fit on top of her head like a crown. Looking closer, she saw that the jewelry was shaped like a dragon winding over flesh.

Nadja looked at his covered face. He did indeed appear bold and strong like a dragon.

"Are you pleased?" he asked confidently when she didn't move. Again, his smile was alluring and light. She could tell by the expression that this was a man who laughed often.

She blinked nervously, trying to erase the image of tight flesh burning into her memory. He took a step forward, moving as if to touch her.

"No," she commanded, her eyes narrowing. Her words stopped him. Her breathing deepened. "Just stay back a moment."

His head tilted to the side, waiting for her command.

Nadja took another deep breath, trying to control her undisciplined emotions and wild heartbeat.

"I don't think there is a need to do any of..." She swallowed nervously and looked at the bath and then the bed. Shivering, she tried to lift her hands to cross protectively over her chest and grew frustrated by the binding straps. With a frown, she tugged the belt off her arms. "I meant to say, I know the tradition of this night is to prove yourself a worthy mate by a display of your..."

As Olek arched a brow, she saw the shifting beneath his mask. His eyes dipped to focus on the way her breasts bounced with her jerking movements. She freed herself from the arm ties and left them to hang at her waist.

Swallowing over her embarrassment, she crossed her arms over her chest to break his gaze, and uttered, "Your prowess."

The grin widened over his amazingly firm lips. Those lips weren't fair. No man should look that delectable. Nadja made a small sound of distress before continuing. She knew he wanted her to choose him for her husband. It wasn't fair. He couldn't really speak until she granted him permission. The only way to grant him permission was to accept him as a husband. Hurting his feelings wasn't a great way to start off their possible life together, so she tried to speak carefully.

"I am telling you, there is no need for that. I am not concerned with..." Nadja felt like kicking herself. The words sounded weak and trembling. Normally she could speak with soft confidence, always reasonable and logical and well-phrased. Her voice came out in hot, breathless pants. What was he doing to her? Her body felt like it was on fire, like she needed to take off her clothes and jump into a snow drift. She started to sweat. Absently, she fanned her face, trying to concentrate. Forgetting where she had left off, she repeated, "I am not concerned with your prowess— *ah!*"

Olek boldly whipped his loincloth from his hips and dropped it to the fur-lined floor.

To find out more about Michelle's books visit www.MichellePillow.com

The Savage King Excerpt

Kirill watched the door to his bedroom open. He'd been sitting in the dark, trying to relieve the stress headache that had built behind his eyes for the last week. The pain started at the base of his skull and radiated up to his temples until he could hardly see straight.

A heavy responsibility had been thrust on his shoulders, a responsibility he really hadn't prepared himself for, the welfare of the Var people. King Attor had not left him in a good position. He'd rallied the people to the brink of war, convinced them that the Draig were their enemy, and even went so far as to attack the Draig royal family.

Kirill wanted to see peace in the land. However, he knew the facts didn't bode well for it. The Draig had a long list of grievances against King Attor and the Var kingdom.

Before his death, the king had ordered an attack on the four Draig princes, all of which ended horribly for the Var. The worst was when Prince Yusef was stabbed in the back, a most cowardly embarrassment for the Var guard who did it. If he hadn't been executed in the Draig prisons, he would've been ostracized from the Var community. Luckily, Prince Yusef survived or they'd already be at battle.

Attor had also arranged for the kidnapping of Yusef's new bride. The Draig Princess Olena had been rescued, or that too would've led to war. The old king had even tried to poison Princess Morrigan, the future Draig queen, on two separate occasions. She too lived. And those were only a few of the offenses Kirill knew about in the few weeks before King Attor's death. He could just imagine what he didn't know.

Kirill sighed, feeling very tired. He'd known since birth that the day would come when he'd be expected to step up and lead the Var as their new king. He just hadn't expected it to be for another hundred or so years. His father had been a hard man, whom he'd foolishly believed was invincible.

"Here kitty, kitty, kitty." His lovely houseguest's whisper drew his complete attention from his heavy thoughts.

Ulyssa bent over like she expected him to answer to the insulting call. He dropped his fingers from his temple into his lap, and a quizzical smile came to his lips. As he watched her, he wasn't sure if he was angered or amused by her words.

"Are you in here, you little furball?" she said, a little louder.

She wore his clothes. Never had the outfit looked sexier. His jaw tightened in masculine interest, as he unabashedly looked her over. All too well did he remember the softness of her body against his and the gentle, offering pleasure of her sweet lips. She'd made soft whimpering noises when he'd touched her, yielding, purring sounds in the back of her throat. Even with the aid of nef, he was surprised by how easily and confidently she melted into him. The Var were wild, passionate people and were drawn to the same qualities in others. He suspected she'd be an untamed lover.

Too bad she'd belonged to his father first. In his mind, that made her completely untouchable though none would dare question his claim if he were to take her to his bed. Technically, by Var law, she belonged to him until he chose to release her. For an insane moment, he thought about keeping her as a lover. He knew he wouldn't, but the thought was entertaining.

Kirill's grin deepened. Ulyssa strode across his home to the bathroom door with an irritated scowl. It was obvious she didn't see him in the darkened corner, watching her. He detected her engaging smell from across the room, the smell of a woman's desire. It stirred his blood, making his limbs heavy with arousal. And, for the first time since his father's death, his headache relieved itself.

"Hum, maybe I'm looking too high. I'm sure there has to be a little cat door here somewhere. Come here, little kitty. Where are you hiding?"

His slight smile fell at her words. It was easy to detect her mocking tone.

"Where's your little kitty door, huh?" Ulyssa whispered to herself, her blue gaze searching around in the dark.

Kirill grimaced in further displeasure. He watched her open the door to his weapons cabinet. Her eyes rounded, and he thought she might take one. She didn't. Instead, she nodded in appreciation before closing the door and continuing her search for an exit.

She stopped at a narrow window by his kitchen doorway. Her neck craned to the side, as she tried to see out over the distance. Kirill knew she looked at the forest. From under her breath, he heard her vehement whisper, "Where exactly did you little fur balls bring me? Ugh, I need to get out of this flea trap, even if I have to fight every one of you cowardly felines to do it. I've fought species twice as big and three times as frightening. A couple of little kitty cats don't scare me."

If this insolent woman wanted to play tough, oh, he'd play. Curling gracefully forward, Kirill shifted before his hands even touched the ground. He let one thick paw land silently on the floor, followed by a second. Short black fur rippled over his tanned flesh, blending him into the shadows. His clothes fell from his body, and he lowered his head as he crept forward. A low sound of warning started in the back of his throat. He was livid.

To find out more about Michelle's books visit www.MichellePillow.com